ONE MOONLIT NIGHT

ONE MOONLIT NIGHT
by T. LLEW JONES

ADAPTED BY GILLIAN CLARKE
ILLUSTRATED BY JAC JONES

PONT BOOKS
1991

i
Mirlo Cai,
Coyan Ifor
a Llaima Mali

First impression — August 1991

ISBN 0 86383 627 5

© the original Welsh text: T. Llew Jones, 1989

© the English text: Gillian Clarke, 1991

© the illustrations: Jac Jones, 1989

The volume is published with the support of the
Welsh Arts Council

Printed at
Gomer Press, Llandysul, Dyfed, Wales

Contents

ONE MOONLIT NIGHT

Guto lived with his father, Siôn Ifan the Tailor, in the village of Llandysul. Like his father, Guto was a tailor and he travelled the countryside with a heavy pack on his back, going from house to house, from farm to farm. On a big farm he might stay for a week or more, making clothes for the whole family as was the custom in those days. His father went with him until he grew too old for travelling.

One moonlit night Guto was on his way home to Llandysul across a lonely moor called Banc-y-Ffordd. The moon shone bright as day, and despite the loneliness of the place Guto was not afraid. He carried a strong stick and hummed a bit of a tune to himself as he strode along.

On Banc-y-Ffordd there is a huge and ancient stone, a famous landmark so old that no one knows its history. As Guto reached the stone something strange happened. Without looking, he stepped in a circle of dark green grass, that special colour by which we know fairy rings from ordinary grass. If you tread in such a ring by day there is no danger, but at night, when the moon is full, the little people use their rings for dancing and you had better watch your step. Poor Guto the Tailor paid dearly for his mistake.

The moment Guto placed two feet into the magic ring he began to dance. Round and round he went, faster and faster. The little people took his hands and whirled him around until he was dizzy, so dizzy he forgot where he was and who he was. He even forgot his own name. The dance whirled on and on until he was a man in a dream bewitched by enchanted music. The dance gathered speed and suddenly he was spun out of the magic circle. At once the sweet music faded and the little people vanished like a morning mist.

He woke feeling stunned, as if he had been in a deep sleep, lying flat on his back on the grass. It was a bright morning, the sun was shining and the shadow of the standing stone fell on the grass beside him. His heart leapt when he saw the stone, because then he knew he was not far from home. He felt weary and his body ached all over, which after such wild dancing

1

was not surprising. Then he remembered he was Guto the Tailor, and he looked about him for his pack and his stick. They were nowhere to be seen, and when he looked down to brush the grass from his clothes he saw that they had turned to rags.

Feeling deeply uneasy Guto got to his feet and began to walk towards Llandysul, but he could hardly move.

'Drat the little people!' he said aloud, and the sound of his own voice startled him. It was high and squeaky and not like his own voice at all.

Slowly he walked towards the bend in the road where Mari Tŷ Clotas' cottage came into view, but when he reached the corner he saw a large, ivy-clad farmhouse. He closed his eyes in case he was dreaming, but when he opened them again the farm still stood where Tŷ Clotas had been. He began to feel afraid, and he looked over his shoulder to see whether the stone was still there. There it was, pointing a black finger against the morning sunlight.

At the farm gate a sheepdog rushed out of the barn baring its teeth and growling. Even this was strange as all the farm dogs knew Guto and ran to welcome him, their tails wagging as he called their names. He remembered Carlo, Mari Tŷ Clotas' dog. Where was he?

Hearing the dog snarl, three small children ran out of the house to stare at Guto in astonishment, and the youngest burst into tears. Their father and mother came out to see what was the matter and they too stared at Guto. The woman shepherded her children into the house and the farmer strode across the yard, an ash stick in his hand. What the farmer saw was an ancient, ragged man with a long white beard, the oldest man he had ever seen.

'Who are you?' he asked.

'Guto, son of Siôn Ifan the Tailor of Llandysul,' the tremulous voice replied. At this the farmer smiled.

'You'd better think of something better than that,' he said.

'What do you mean?'

'Well, my friend, I was born and bred in Llandysul and there is no tailor there called Guto, nor Siôn Ifan either.'

'Oh dear!' said Guto. 'What is going on? What is happening to me? I was dancing on the moor on my way home then I remember feeling very strange.'

The man smiled again.

'Dancing! I'd like to have seen that, old man!'

'Old man! I'm young! Twenty years old!'

'Twenty! You're a hundred if you're a day!' said the farmer in astonishment. A breath of wind blew Guto's long hair across his eyes. He caught a strand of hair in his hand, and it was as white as snow.

Seeing Guto's stunned expression, the farmer began to feel he'd been unkind to the old fellow.

'Come into the house and have something to eat,' he said. 'Then you can go to Llandysul to look for Siôn Ifan the Tailor.'

The farmer's wife watched with disapproval as her husband brought the strange person into the kitchen, but she placed a cup of milk before him and began to cut bread and butter, and Guto sat down to eat.

'Where is Mari Tŷ Clotas?' he asked suddenly. The couple exchanged glances and the farmer tapped his head and winked.

'I'd like to know where Mari Tŷ

Clotas is. And Carlo,' said Guto. 'And, come to think, where is Tŷ Clotas?'

Guto began to go over his adventure to himself. 'I was coming home over the moor—it was a fine, moonlit night—and I began to dance—to dance with the little people—'

'Little people!' said the woman. 'No one believes in them any more.'

'There is an old woman in Llandysul who believes in the little people. Would you like to go and see her?' asked the farmer.

The farmer and his wife were glad of an excuse to get rid of the old man.

'I must go to Llandysul,' said Guto, getting up from the table.

'I'll take you,' said the farmer.

They left the house and walked along the steep, winding road until Llandysul came into view among the woods on the banks of the Teifi. Guto stared. What a change! It was bigger, the streets were full of strangers, and the houses looked different. But the church was still there, the old stone bridge still crossed the river and there was the oak tree in whose branches he had played as a child.

Guto and the farmer reached the house where the old woman who believed in the little people lived. She sat in the kitchen on the settle, her cheeks yellow as old paper. The farmer explained that he had brought a visitor, an old man called Guto who said he was the son of Siôn Ifan the Tailor.

'Impossible,' said the old woman. 'I remember my father used to speak of him when I was a girl, but he'd be over a hundred years old by now. Wait a minute now.' The old woman sat muttering to herself. 'There was a story about Siôn Ifan the Tailor—he was related to my father—what was the story! I can't remember.'

'Don't upset yourself, old woman,' said the farmer, worried that he might have to listen to a long, rambling tale. 'I only brought him to talk to you about the little people.'

The old woman peered at Guto with her watery blue eyes.

'You believe in the little people! Ah! Now I remember. The story of Siôn Ifan the Tailor! Talking about the little people brings it back. It's the story of Guto, Siôn Ifan's son, to tell the truth.'

The farmer was about to leave as she spoke, but he paused to listen.

'Guto was a tailor like his father and he went round the farms making clothes. One moonlit night he was on his way home to Llandysul across the moor, but he never reached home and no one ever saw him again. They found his pack and stick by the standing stone on the moor, but he'd disappeared as if the earth had swallowed him. Some people said robbers killed him and hid his body, but his father and I believed that he stepped in a fairy ring on the night of a full moon.'

'Yes!' wheezed Guto. 'That's it! I remember now. I stepped into a fairy ring and here I am, all alone, a hundred years later, in the midst of strangers. I have no home, no kith, no kin, nothing.'

'Yes, you still have family,' said the old woman. 'You forget Siôn Ifan was related to my father. So you are related to me and there is a home here with me if you want it.'

So Guto moved in to the cottage by the river Teifi, and he and the old woman lived happily enough together to the end of their days.

Each evening in winter Guto

would sit on the settle by the fire, and in summer he leaned on the stone bridge and gazed into the tumbling waters of the river. There he would tell his story to anyone who would listen—a strange tale of standing stones and fairy rings, of sweet music and wild dancing one moonlit night, a hundred years ago.

OLD COPENHAGEN

Not far from Newtown in Powys there was a beautiful mansion where a rich family lived. Once, in the depths of winter, the family went on a long journey leaving their house and treasures in the care of Alis the maid, Rhisiart the farmhand and Edward the servant boy.

Edward was a lazy, mischievous lad. He had an old-fashioned gun bought from an old soldier in the village, and he used it to shoot crows in the mansion grounds. The gun bore the wonderful name of 'Copenhagen', and this, and its dark, unknown history, made the gun Edward's greatest treasure.

Late one afternoon Alis was in the kitchen spinning, when a pedlar knocked at the door. On his back he carried a huge, shapeless pack. Alis was used to the sight of passing pedlars, their shoulders weighed down with bundles, but never such a large heavy, lumpy load as this one.

Alis welcomed the packman into the comfort of the warm kitchen. Carefully the pedlar lowered his enormous load to the floor in a corner of the room and chatted amusingly to the maid. She had never in her life heard such a witty, sweet-talking man. His flattery was enough to turn a girl's head, but Alis was a sensible girl.

At last, when the pedlar asked for a bed for the night, Alis refused. 'What!' he cried. 'Are you refusing shelter to a weary traveller? It is almost dark out there. I've walked a long way and I'm very tired . . .'

Still Alis shook her head.

'I'll give you a present. The finest shawl in my pack if I can stay tonight.'

A fine new shawl from the pedlar's pack! Alis hesitated. Then she remembered her master's warning that she should never let a stranger into the house at night when he was away. She had promised, so once more she shook her head.

The pedlar saw that she had made up her mind.

'All right,' he said, 'I'll have to find lodgings elsewhere. But at least let me leave my heavy pack here until the morning. I am too tired to carry it any further.'

Alis agreed to let him leave his

6

pack, and when he asked if he might put it somewhere safer than the kitchen, she led him to the parlour which no one used when the family was away. He eased the pack carefully onto two chairs and went on his way. By now night had fallen on the house, its neat gardens and its tangle of dark woods.

Alis returned to her spinning but she could not get that strange, lumpy parcel out of her mind. She opened the parlour door and went in. The huge pack lay slumped on two chairs where the pedlar had lowered it. Alis stood a long time staring at it. Then—impossible!—she could have sworn it moved, like something breathing. A shock ran through her and she felt her hair stand on end. She was trembling like a flame in a draught as she reached the kitchen. The candle fell from her hand and went out. Darkness and terror overpowered her and she began to shout, 'Rhisiart! Rhisiart!'

There was no answer. From somewhere she gathered courage to run from the kitchen across the dark yard to the barn where Rhisiart was working by the light of a candle.

'Oh! Rhisiart!' she cried. 'Come to the house. Quick, Rhisiart bach!'

The farmhand was a cautious man. 'What is the trouble, Alis?' he asked calmly.

'The pedlar's left his pack in the parlour.'

'Well? Nothing to get upset about. He'll be back in the morning to fetch it no doubt.'

'But listen, Rhisiart bach! There's something alive in the pack. Come on! Hurry!'

When the old man heard 'something alive' he put aside his work and without haste he went into the house with Alis.

As Alis and Rhisiart were lighting candles in the dark kitchen, Edward the servant boy appeared from nowhere.

When he heard talk of the big pack and the 'something alive' inside it, he said eagerly,

'Well, here's a good chance to give Copenhagen some target practice.'

'Hold your tongue, silly boy,' said the farmhand angrily.

Before they could blink Edward had gone to the parlour, a candle in his hand. He was back in a moment.

'It's alive!' he cried.

'What's the matter with you, boy? Have you lost your wits like Alis here?'

'I saw it move. I'm going to shoot it, Alis.'

'No, Ned bach. Don't be in such a hurry,' Rhisiart warned.

The boy realised that Alis half-approved of the idea, though she said nothing. It was enough for the boy. He was off to fetch his gun, and soon returned with Copenhagen in his hands. He ran to the parlour, the other two hard on his heels. He lifted the gun to his shoulder, looked down the long barrel, aimed it at the bundle, and fired.

The gunshot rang through every room of the house and from the pack came the sound of a low cry. As the three terrified servants watched, blood began to seep through the cloth and a scarlet pool began to form on the carpet.

Of the three it was Edward who was most afraid. He had been a big man as he talked of firing Copenhagen, but when he heard the cry and saw the blood he wanted to run home to his mother. Slowly, limply the bundle slid from the two chairs onto the ground where it slumped, quite still. They looked at each other, appalled, not knowing what to do.

It was Rhisiart the old farmhand who found enough sense and courage to approach the blood-stained bundle. He took out his pocket knife and began to cut the parcel open. Inside lay a young man, quite dead, and beside him a long, rapier-sharp knife and four pistols.

They knew at once that Edward had shot a robber with his old Copenhagen, a robber smuggled into the house by the charming, silver-tongued pedlar. The farmhand found a whistle in the dead man's pocket, and at once they understood the villain's plot. In the dead of night the young man in the pack would have freed himself, unlocked the door and whistled for his accomplices as a sign that the coast was clear. Once inside the house they would have robbed it of all its treasures.

The three servants returned to the kitchen to decide what to do next. Out there in the darkness bandits were lying in wait for a signal. They must summon help. Edward the servant boy crept out by the back door and ran silently through the night to a neighbouring farm to tell their story and beg for help. The news spread like fire through stubble and soon a band of farmers arrived at the mansion ready and angry enough to kill the bandits.

The little group inside the house waited all night, but nothing happened. As dawn broke Edward gave one sharp call on the whistle.

At once they heard the sound of horses' hooves galloping through the woods close to the house. In the grey half-light of dawn the shadowy figures of armed riders appeared between the trees. Edward lifted his old Copenhagen to his shoulder, and as the first horseman broke from the cover of the wood, he fired. The rider twisted and fell to the ground, and his horse trotted away trailing the reins. At once the other horsemen veered away and galloped back into the forest.

That day the gentleman came home to hear how his house and treasures had been saved from an armed band of robbers by Alis the maid, Rhisiart the farmhand, Edward the servant boy, and old Copenhagen.

The Red Bandits of Mawddwy

Four hundred years ago near the village of Dinas Mawddwy, a band of robbers known as the Red Bandits, lived in secret caves in the ravines under the dense, dark forests that covered the mountainsides.

The bandits used to lurk among the trees at the roadside, and when rich travellers passed that way they sprang from their hiding place to attack and rob the travellers of their jewellery and money. Then they disappeared like shadows into the forest and no one knew where they had gone, because they alone knew how to find the entrances to the secret caves. The bandits were as elusive as ghosts, and everyone was terrified of them.

At that time a powerful nobleman called Baron Owen lived in Dolgellau. He was a judge at the court, and he was famous for his hard-hearted treatment of criminals. They say he was more likely to hang an accused man than show him mercy.

Like everyone else in Wales he had heard of the Red Bandits, and he was enraged by the stories of their daring attacks on travellers.

'This is a terrible business,' he thought. 'Every one of these villains must be caught and hanged.'

The problem was that very little was known about the bandits, and no one knew of the secret gullies and caverns in the forest. Who they were, and where they came from, was a mystery.

One morning as Christmas was coming and sheets of snow lay over the land, the Baron got out of bed, stretched himself, and gazed out of his window.

'Ha!' cried the Baron. 'Now is the time to hunt the Red Bandits! If they try to escape through the woods they will leave their guilty tracks in the snow.'

At once he set about gathering a band of soldiers and local noblemen, all as keen as he was to be rid of the bandits. Soon a troop of horsemen was galloping through the snow towards Dinas Mawddwy. It was a cold and silent morning, the only sounds the clink of soldiers' armour and the muffled drumming of hooves in the snow.

Before long they reached the dark forest of Dinas Mawddwy where the bandits lived. All was quiet as the grave, with a fine layer of snow covering everything and not a sign of human life anywhere.

Baron Owen led his troop into the woods. There was something very creepy about the forest, and some of the men began to wish they had stayed warm and safe at home.

In the heart of the forest they found the bandits' deserted camp with signs of disturbed snow and the hot ashes of a fire. The bandits had fled even deeper into the woods leaving their tracks printed sharply in the freshly fallen snow.

'After them!' cried the Baron.

The Baron's men followed the tangled chains of footprints on the snow-covered ground, deeper and deeper into the trees, and at last they trapped the bandits at the foot of a sheer cliff, bound them hand and foot and brought them before Baron Owen, who was standing beside his horse in a small clearing.

'Hang the whole mob of them!' demanded the Baron. One by one the bandits were hanged from the trees that surrounded the clearing.

Two young boys, hardly fifteen years old, were among those captured by the soldiers. They stood with their mother in the middle of the glade. The soldiers were reluctant to hang such young and innocent boys with the rest of the robbers, so they went to the Baron and asked him, 'Should these two boys be set free?'

'Hang them!' shouted the Baron without hesitation.

When their mother heard these words she fell at the Baron's feet imploring him not to kill her two sons who had never harmed anyone. Her tears fell scalding into the snow.

'Have mercy!' she cried, lifting her arms to entreat the Baron. He stared scornfully down on her and turned on his heel, making a gesture to the soldiers that they should get on with the job. Within two minutes the young brothers were hanging side by side from the bough of a great oak tree, a rope about each throat. In her anguish the boys' mother ran after the Baron shouting,

'Vengeance! There will be vengeance, Baron Owen.' Then she turned and vanished into the trees with a scream shrill enough to freeze the soldiers' blood.

The Baron heard her but he took no notice. He felt well satisfied that he had outwitted, captured and hanged most of the notorious Red Bandits of Mawddwy, and he thought with pleasure that it would make him even more famous and even more feared as a stern judge.

He and his friends rode happily home to Dolgellau through Bwlch-yr-Oerddrws, the gap of the cold gate, and that night at the Baron's mansion there was feasting and drinking and carousing and laughter until the early hours of the morning. Out in the dark forest of Dinas Mawddwy, the bodies of the bandits hung silently in the moonlight.

Time passed and the merciless Baron Owen and his cruel punishments grew more notorious than ever. Once more, it was winter and Christmas was coming and the Baron and half a dozen servants were returning home on horseback through the forest of Dinas Mawddwy. They hurried because it was growing dark and the trees threw deep purple shadows over the snow.

Suddenly a flight of arrows whistled from the heart of the wood and Baron Owen fell from his white horse and lay on the earth groaning with pain, an arrow in his eye. The bandits rushed out of the trees and crowded round the nobleman lying wounded on the ground. His servants fled in fear but there was no escape for the Baron. One of the bandits raised his arm in the air to stab the Baron through the heart, and in the moment before the dagger struck, the Baron saw a woman staring down on him, a bitter smile on her face. It was the mother of the two young boys he had hanged from the old oak tree.

There are no longer any Red Bandits in Mawddwy. But as long as there are travellers on that road, and as long as Welsh is spoken, their story will be told.

Daughters of the Sea

The saddest sound in the world is the cry of a gull. As it circles the restless sea, or flies over the land, it sounds like someone grieving forever for something lost. What is the secret of the seagull's sorrow?

In a mansion near New Quay in Ceredigion there lived a gentleman with his three beautiful daughters, Branwen, Gwenllian and Llio. Their hair was the colour of gorse-flowers, their eyes like the air of a June day, their skin pale as sea-foam. The sisters were famous for their beauty throughout the land and young men travelled from far and wide just to look at them.

Often in summer the sisters walked on the beach at the edge of the tide and heard the waves whisper their names as they broke on the shore, 'Branwen — Gwenllian — Llio.'

Rumour of their beauty spread across land and sea and eventually reached the ears of Dylan the sea-god. The waves brought the news to his crystal palace under the ocean where the treasures of all the ships ever lost at sea were kept, and where the mermaids lived. The palace walls were built of coral and its windows were glazed with pearl. Sea-trees and sea-weeds grew in its gardens and rainbow-coloured fish darted among the fronds of its branches. It was the waves, not the wind, that stirred the foliage in the sea-god's garden.

'Branwen — Gwenllian — Llio— the most beautiful girls on earth,' whispered the waves into his ear. Tide after tide the waves brought the same message to Dylan until at last he decided to see them for himself.

One summer evening, when the girls were walking on the white sand, Dylan swam into the shallow waters of the bay and lifted his head to look at them. The girls watched the waves lapping and retreating again and again on the shore, and they felt no sense of dread, and had no reason to feel afraid. They did not notice the sea-god with his beard of seaweed and his hair of foam encrusted with sea-shells rising among the restless waters of the bay. Dylan gazed at them for a long time. The waves had not lied. He'd never seen such beauty before and he longed to take the three girls to live with him in his deep sea palace of coral and pearl. At last he slipped slowly and thoughtfully back to the bottom of the sea.

After that day Dylan often came at sunset to watch the sisters walking on the beach, and every time he saw them he longed more and more for their company. At last he decided to steal them.

One night he called the winds and the waves to him. They were his servants and they obeyed at once.

That night the fiercest storm New

14

Quay had ever known raged out of the Atlantic and struck the little town. The wind howled. The waves hurled themselves higher and higher against the cliffs. The sea scattered the boats on the shore and flooded the fishermen's cottages. The tide rose so high that at last the waves were licking the threshold of the mansion on the cliff where the three sisters lived with their father.

Then, on the highest wave of all, Dylan rode out of the sea and stood listening at the window of the mansion house.

In the sitting-room the sisters sat by the fire. Llio played her harp, Gwenllian was plaiting her hair and Branwen worked at her embroidery. They listened to the storm and Gwenllian said nervously,

'I've never known the wind and sea as wild as this. I'm scared.'

'Tut!' answered Branwen impatiently. 'We are used to storms here. Just listen to the harp.'

She put down her embroidery and turned to listen to Llio who was playing an old sweet air to the sound of waves drumming. Out in the storm Dylan stood listening, enchanted.

The melody came to an end and Llio looked up suddenly.

'Did you hear that?' she said. 'Someone's calling.'

She left the room, went to the front door and opened it. She stepped onto the porch and felt the full force of the wind as the door slammed shut behind her.

Time passed and she did not come back. Branwen and Gwenllian looked at each other uneasily.

'I'll go and see what's happened,' said Branwen. She went outside into the storm and the front door slammed behind her.

Gwenllian waited alone in the room but she could not sit still while her sisters were outside so she opened the door and called their names into the storm. 'Branwen! Llio!' There was no answer. The wind grabbed her and lifted her over the threshold. She felt waves flowing about her feet, spray drenching her hair and the watery hand of the sea-god on her shoulder. Then she fainted.

By dawn the storm had died away. The old man searched the house for his daughters but there was no sign of them anywhere. He went from room to room calling their names. No one answered so he called his servants.

'Go and find my daughters. Something has happened to them. Do not come back without news of them!' Tears filled his eyes.

The servants went on their errand. They searched every nook and cranny but found no sign of the girls. Late that afternoon the oldest servant came back from the village.

'Is there any news?' asked the old man eagerly. The servant answered.

'Down in the village I was talking to a fisherman.'

'Yes?'

'He said he was out last night when the storm was at its worst. He was seeing to his boat. He had a lantern, and by the harbour wall he saw yellow hair in the sea.'

'Yellow hair!' the old man leapt to his feet. 'My daughters' hair! The sea has taken them! They are drowned!'

No one could comfort him and for days he wandered alone on the beach calling pitifully,

'Branwen! Gwenllian! Llio!'

The villagers were terrified, and children were not allowed to play on the beach any more.

15

Meanwhile, under the sea, in the sea-god's palace, the girls sobbed and sulked.

'Sing to me!' said Dylan.

'How can we sing without air and sunlight?' cried Llio.

Dylan was already sorry for what he had done.

'Please let us go. Please!' pleaded Gwenllian.

Dylan frowned. 'I'm afraid I can't,' he said. 'It's impossible. Once you belong to the sea you can't ever leave it. I have no power to take you home.'

The waves told Dylan how the old gentleman walked the beach day after day calling his daughters.

At dusk Dylan swam into the shallow waters of the bay. There he saw the old man walking alone and heard him calling 'Branwen! Gwenllian! Llio!' over and over again. Hearing such sorrow, Dylan felt ashamed of stealing the girls. He wanted to take them home to their father but he did not know how. Only a magician had such power. Then he had an idea. Could the girls belong both to the sea and to the land? He would try to make this possible. Anything was better than hearing them sob under the sea forever.

Next morning, when the old man took his usual walk on the beach calling his daughters' names— 'Branwen! Gwenllian! Llio!'—three white gulls flew inland from the sea. The sun shone on their gleaming wings and on their foam-white breasts. The three birds alighted gently on the old man's shoulders and he knew at once they were his daughters. He stroked their soft feathers and talked to them tenderly.

Years went by and every day the three white gulls came to the shore or to the house on the cliff. Every day they kept the old man company and as night fell they flew back to the sea.

That, so the old story says, is why the saddest sound in the world is the cry of a gull. On land she is troubled with a longing for the sea. At sea she aches with a yearning for the land. She belongs nowhere, and every night and every day she cries for what she has lost.

THE TAPPERS

The old Cardiganshire lead-mines closed a long time ago, and only waste-heaps and derelict buildings remain to show where they once were.

A hundred years ago something strange happened in one of those old mines.

In Cwmsymlog the lead was all used up. Although the miners searched with pick and shovel in every likely place underground, they could not find a vein of lead ore. The masters threatened to close the mine, refusing to pay the miners' wages if there was no more lead to be found.

One Saturday morning one of the masters came to tell the men that the mine would be closed at the end of the day. The miners worked their last shift with heavy hearts, and sadly made their way home.

'We knew they'd close Cwmsymlog,' said one miner to another. 'No one has heard the tappers in Cwmsymlog for years. If you don't hear the tappers you'll never find the lead. It's finished.'

'There's enough lead,' said an old miner, 'if only we could find it. If you ask me the tappers are angry with Cwmsymlog miners and that's why they won't show us the lead.'

'Tut! Rubbish!' shouted a young miner.

Deio Bach of Ty'n Ddôl was ten years old and he had just started work with his father at Cwmsymlog mine. He listened without a word to the miners' talk. He had heard of the tappers, of course. Everyone knew about the little men who lived under the ground and looked after the metals in the rock, tapping to show the miners the way to the veins of lead. Few had ever seen them but many talked of hearing them a long time ago.

On the way home Deio asked his father.

'Why hasn't anyone heard the tappers for a long time?'

His father shook his head. He was feeling too sad to speak. How would he buy food and clothes for his family now the mine had closed?

That night the hearth at Ty'n Ddôl was a sorrowful place. Deio's father looked worried and his mother sniffed and wiped the tears from her eyes.

Deio went to bed early but he could not sleep for thinking of the dark underground passages and the strange little men who lived there. Was it true that they were angry with the miners?

Sunday was a fine October day and Deio's mother had cooked a good Sunday dinner. She had picked blackberries on the hills on Saturday afternoon and had made a large blackberry tart. When she took it, hot and golden out of the oven, Deio had a big slice. It was his mother's speciality and in Deio's opinion the most delicious dish in the world.

After dinner his mother and father went out to visit a sick neighbour, leaving Deio alone in the house.

He thought and thought about the tappers. If only they would help, the miners' troubles would be over and they could all be happy again.

Then he had a brilliant idea.

He went into the pantry where his mother had put the blackberry tart, cut a large slice and took a clean cloth which lay folded beside it on the cold slate slab.

After wrapping the tart carefully in the cloth he went out of the house and down the winding track to the mine.

As it was Sunday there was no one about and soon he reached the mouth of the tunnel which led into Cwm-symlog mine.

With a glance over his shoulder to make sure no one saw him, Deio walked into the black hole. As he saw darkness looming in front of him he realised that he had forgotten to bring a candle and he almost turned back, but after a moment's hesitation he stepped into the tunnel. Soon the daylight behind him glimmered and disappeared. His foot stumbled now and then on the uneven ground and he almost fell. Once he struck his head on a rock as the tunnel turned a corner.

The deserted mine was as dark and silent as a tomb. Deio stood listening but he heard nothing but the wind sighing in the labyrinth of underground tunnels.

Suddenly he stood still and spoke into the silence.

'Little Men,' he said, and his voice echoing eerily in the shaft made him jump. 'Little Men, are you there? Can you hear me? I've brought you a slice of Mam's blackberry tart.'

He stopped to listen but no answer came from the darkness, only the echo of his own voice fading away like ripples in a bottomless pool when a stone is dropped into it.

'Are you angry with the miners? They still believe in you.'

'You . . . you . . . you . . .' came back from the silence of the pit.

'I've brought you some of Mam's blackberry tart to prove we still believe in you. They've closed the mine. Please help us.'

The silence was vast. It filled the hollowed-out heart of the mountain. Were little ears listening somewhere in the darkness? Deio put the slice of tart on a ledge and turned to walk towards the daylight.

For a while he walked in the dark expecting to see the mouth of the tunnel at any moment, but no daylight appeared so he sat on a rock to rest.

How on earth was he going to find his way out of the mine? He got to his feet and walked on and on, stumbling several times, but no light broke the gloom. He now knew he was lost and he sat down on a boulder for a long time and began to cry quietly. Time passed and at last he closed his eyes and was soon asleep.

Deio woke suddenly to see the tunnel filled with brilliant blue light. He thought his father had come to rescue him, but instead of his father he saw a very small man sitting on the rock beside him carrying a tiny lantern which made the tunnel as bright as if a full moon were shining into it. The little man had a long white beard and his hands were as horny as the hands of Cwmsymlog miners, and he carried a pick and a shovel, if such tiny things could be called picks and shovels.

'Thank you for the blackberry tart,' said the little man.

'That's alright,' said Deio shyly.

'It's the best tart we've ever tasted.'

Deio smiled. He was proud to hear his mother's tart so highly praised.

'Because you believe in us we'll help the Cwmsymlog miners. Follow me.'

He picked up his little lamp in one hand and his pick and shovel in the other and off he went down the tunnel with Deio following close behind. After a while the little man stopped. 'Listen!' he said.

For the first time in his life Deio heard the tappers. The sound was like the faraway rhythm of picks working somewhere in the depths of the earth, the sound the Cwmsymlog miners had long listened for in vain.

'The tappers!' cried Deio, his heart thumping with excitement.

The little man walked on and Deio followed close behind. The tapping came closer until at last Deio stood near to the source of the sound, but where were the little workmen? Deio saw no one.

'The lead,' said the little man, pointing at the wall.

'Here?'

'Yes, here, behind this rock-face. I'll make a mark on the rock so that you'll remember where to dig.'

He put his tiny lantern on the ground and made a long groove in the stone with his pick.

'See that?' he said. 'That's where you must dig for the lead.'

Suddenly the little man vanished, the tunnel grew dark and Deio was alone again, afraid and disappointed because although he knew where the lead was, he was lost and could not take the good news to the miners. He was hungry and thirsty and very cold.

Some time later, it seemed like hours, he thought he heard voices in the distance, but silence fell again. An hour passed and he was certain he could see a faraway beam of light. He feared he'd imagined it, but it came closer and he heard voices, louder this time. He recognised his father's voice and shouted as loudly as he could. 'Dad! Dad!' Footsteps came closer and soon his father was putting his arms around him in relief and joy.

When he and his wife came home to the empty house they asked neighbours if they had seen Deio. Someone had noticed him walking in the direction of the mine, and soon his

worried mother and father had set out to search for him.

That night by the fire Deio told his story and before dawn the next day his father and three other miners followed Deio into the old mine.

After a long search they came to the rock-face with the tiny mark on it cut by the little man's pick. There the men picked and shovelled for hours and at last they uncovered a rich vein of lead ore

At once they took the news to the masters. Next morning all the miners of Cwmsymlog were back at work, whistling and hammering, and everyone was happy again, especially Deio Bach of Ty'n Ddôl.

The HARPIST

There was once a gentleman called Einion who lived with his wife Elen in the county of Cardiganshire. Einion was a rich man but he was kind and generous, and his beautiful wife Elen was as warm-hearted as he was. They worked hard to help the people of Tregaron, and no poor or sick person was ever turned away from their door.

Tregaron was a happy place to live in those days, and much of this contentment was due to Elen and Einion.

Einion was a fine harper and no one entertained company at the big house better than he as he sang the old Welsh songs to the tune of his harp. The happiest evenings of all were when Einion brought out his great harp, for then he made the sweetest music in the world. When the great harp was played no one sang—they only listened, and when at last the harp fell silent everyone went happily home to bed, convinced that Einion was the greatest harper Wales had ever known.

The years went by and one day Elen noticed that her husband was looking pale and thin.

At first Elen said nothing, but days passed and Einion's health grew worse. From week to week he grew more haggard, and he developed a dry cough that troubled him night and day. The great harp stood under a shroud of dust in the corner and there were no more parties at the big house.

Elen sent for the best doctor in the land to visit Einion, but for all his skill the doctor could not cure him. By now everyone thought Einion was dying and the people of Tregaron were heavy-hearted.

At last an old doctor told Einion

23

that the only hope of a cure for his illness was a sea voyage. He thought the fresh salt air of the sea would cure Einion's cough and improve his appetite, then he would grow strong again and his health would return.

Einion thought about the old doctor's advice. He did not want to leave his dear wife and his country, but Elen persuaded him to think of his health, and at last he decided to make a sea voyage as the doctor had advised.

Einion boarded a ship at Fishguard and sailed south and after only a few weeks at sea he began to feel better. Already he was stronger and soon his cough was quite cured. He felt like a new man, full of energy again, and he longed for the day when the ship would turn its prow for home. At first he did not fret, but waited patiently for the ship to make its homeward voyage. Then one day, as the ship was sailing through the Mediterranean Sea, it was attacked by pirates, fierce-looking men who took the crew and passengers prisoner, ransacked the ship and stole everything on board.

A year passed and Elen and the people of Tregaron waited in vain for news of Einion. By this time a second year had passed, and Elen lost all hope of ever seeing her husband again. Everyone feared that his ship had been wrecked and Einion drowned.

Tregaron grieved for Einion. Elen was such a beautiful woman that gentlemen came from far and near to try to persuade her to marry again, but she thought only of the husband she loved.

A third year passed without news of him and, at last, Elen agreed to marry one of the wealthiest men in Cardiganshire. A great marriage feast

was prepared for the eve of the wedding, and after supper the guests asked for a tune on the harp. Among the guests there were several who could play, and someone remembered that Einion's old harp still stood in the corner of the hall. No one had touched it for more than three years and its cover was furred with grey dust.

They uncovered the harp and carried it to the centre of the hall where one by one the harpers tried to play it, but only a harsh, discordant sound came from its strings.

That evening a shabby old tramp came knocking at the kitchen door of the big house to ask for food and a bed for the night. One of the maids gave him supper and a chair by the stove in the kitchen, and from where he sat he could hear the harsh noise of the harp in the hall.

'That harp needs tuning,' he said to the maid.

'There's no one in the house who can tune it,' said the maid.

'I can tune it,' said the tramp.

'Are you a harper?'

His expression was strange and his eyes full of light.

'I was once a harper,' he said, 'and I have not forgotten.'

The maid went to tell Elen the news and the tramp was sent for. He was invited to play the harp for the guests, so he sat on a chair and tuned the strings one by one. Then he drew his fingers lightly and swiftly over the strings and music filled the hall, not the voice of the crow this time but of the nightingale. People stopped talking and turned to listen to the music that came swelling and falling from the harp. Who was the mysterious, shabby musician? Was there ever such a harper?

When the tune came to an end the harper paused, then began to play an old Welsh air which Elen knew well.

'My house, my harp, my fire.'

At once she understood. She stood up and turned to face the enthralled guests.

'Friends,' she said. 'Einion, my husband, has come home. Will you please leave us now?'

The guests rose. One by one they left the great hall until Elen and Einion were alone. What happiness they felt!

After three years of imprisonment sailing the seas as a slave on the pirate ship, Einion had escaped to find his long way home to Wales disguised as a tramp, lean and shabby, but healthy and strong again.

Einion cast off his rags and dressed in the clothes of the gentleman he really was. In the big house and the town of Tregaron everyone rejoiced. Never again was the harp allowed to lie silent under a veil of dust in the corner of the hall.

THE SHAGGY GIANT

Near Hafod-y-Llan in Snowdonia the river Erch falls over a cliff into a deep, dark pool, and after heavy rain it tumbles in a glittering torrent of watersnakes and rainbows to break on the rocks far below.

Behind the waterfall, hidden by the spindrift that hangs perpetually in the air, is a secret cave discovered long ago by chance by three young boys.

The people of Nantgwynant were troubled by a mysterious thief who came at night to steal their chickens and sheep and the milk and butter from the dairies. The robber crept so swiftly and silently in the darkness that no one had ever seen him clearly and there had been neither sight nor sound of him for a long time.

People were terrified of the dark, and they put strong locks on their doors and kept fierce dogs to stop the thief breaking in.

All their precautions were in vain. They could not keep the thief out. He grew more and more daring but no one ever saw anything more than a shadow vanishing into the night.

One summer dusk a shepherd from Hafod-y-Llan was returning home from looking after his flock on the mountain. The sun had almost set and the village of Hafod-y-Llan was already in shadow when he saw a huge, shaggy man sitting on a rock overlooking the valley. The man's hair and beard were red and his arms and legs were covered with long flame-red hair which glowed in the last rays of the setting sun.

The shepherd's heart thumped because he knew he must pass close behind the man on the rock on his way down to Hafod-y-Llan. He crept quietly, crouching low, afraid that

27

the creature would turn and see him at any moment.

The giant was too busy watching what was going on in Hafod-y-Llan to notice the shepherd creeping close behind him. The shepherd arrived home safely and ran to his cottage window to look back at the strange figure sitting on the rock silhouetted against the clear evening sky, sure that this was the monster who had caused them so much trouble and fear for so long.

The farmers of Hafod-y-Llan gathered their servants and dogs and set out at once to catch the thief, but when the shaggy giant saw men and dogs coming towards him he ran like a hound through the heather and gorse and suddenly vanished. The men searched the mountain and kept watch late into the night in case the robber returned. At last they gave up, certain that he could not be hiding anywhere on the mountain, and they went home to Hafod-y-Llan where light, warmth and supper welcomed them.

News spread that the people of Hafod-y-Llan had seen a shaggy giant, and other shepherds began to keep watch on the mountain. Soon others saw the giant basking in the warmth of the heather-covered slopes. Once he was dozing in the sun, his thick hair camouflaging him from the shepherds, when a dog wandered close to him, raised its hackles and barked. He sprang to his feet and leapt from crag to crag. The shepherds were amazed at his speed. They had never seen any man run so fast over the scree and stones of the mountain. There was no hope of catching him. No dog alive could win a race against such a monster and soon he had vanished once again.

Time passed and again and again the robber returned in the night to steal sheep. Sometimes blood was found on the heather where he had made his kill. On lonely farms, a long way from their neighbours, families lived in fear, children would not go to sleep at night and mothers lay listening for strange noises.

The shaggy giant looked so wild and ran so fast over the hills that people began to believe he was no ordinary human being, but an evil spirit.

What could they do? The people decided to ask the help of a magician who lived in a cave on the far side of the mountain.

'You must find a pure red hound,' the magician said. 'If there is even one black or white hair on his body he won't do, but if you can find a hound with a perfect red coat, he will outrun the giant.'

The people of Nantgwynant searched everywhere for a perfect red hound and at last they found one. They took the dog to the mountain many times without seeing the robber, then one afternoon they saw him sitting on the open slopes. They set the red dog on his trail, and what a race followed! No man had ever run so fast over the slopes yet the dog almost caught up with him. As he reached the ridge at the top of the cliffs, the dog at his heels, suddenly the robber disappeared over the edge of the precipice. The red dog stopped at the edge, whining.

When the shepherds reached the foot of the cliff they were sure they would find the body of the dead giant. But only stones and boulders lay beside the turbulent waters of the river. He had escaped again.

Now they were sure he was an evil

spirit because even the red hound could not catch him.

Beside the mountain track above the village stood a cottage called Ty'n-yr-Owallt where a shepherd and his wife lived. One spring night when the shepherd was out late on the mountain looking after his flock of ewes and new lambs, a strange thing happened.

His wife was at home alone, night was falling and she was feeling nervous. She opened the door and looked out towards the dark slopes, hoping to see the swinging lantern her husband carried, but the mountain was black and empty. She went back inside, closed the door and drew the heavy iron bolt into place, thankful that the windows were too small to let a giant in. Then she lit a candle and sat by the fire to wait for her husband. Sometimes she tilted her head to listen, but all was silent. Why was he so late? An hour passed and he still had not come, when she heard a sound at the door. Was it the wind, a footstep on the path, or an animal breathing? She rose from her chair in fear. Something was panting hoarsely and scratching at the door.

She was sure it was the giant and looked quickly around for something to defend herself. In the corner stood a heavy axe with a sharp blade which her husband used to split logs for the fire. She took the axe in her hand.

The noise grew louder and the door shook. It was made of heavy oak and the lock and bar were strong, so she hoped the creature could not burst it open. A moment later the animal noise grew to a shriek and the creature had split the door timbers. She heard the strong oak splintering and saw a hairy arm come through the hole in the door. In her terror she

raised the axe above her head and brought it down with all her strength on the hairy arm. She saw the monster's hand fall to the floor and heard a terrible screech outside and the sound of feet running away. For a long time she stood staring in horror at the hairy hand on the floor, then, feeling very lonely, she began to cry.

Before long her husband arrived home and when he heard his wife's story and saw the hairy hand he decided they should go at once to Hafod-y-Llan to tell the villagers what his brave wife had done.

When they heard the story the villagers were very excited. 'This is our chance,' they said. 'In the morning we'll follow him. There'll be blood on the grass and heather to lead us to his lair.'

Next morning a group of men went to the cottage on the mountain track and there was blood on the threshold and on the grass as they had expected. The men followed the trail of blood over the stones, expecting to find the body of the giant at any moment. The drops of blood led them to the waterfall where all traces stopped, washed away by the waters.

'He's run through the waterfall,' they shouted. 'What is on the other side?'

Three young boys ran behind the waterfall and there, behind the shining curtain of water was the mouth of a secret cave. It was too dark to see down into the cave but they could hear the sound of loud snoring. Too scared to go inside the cave, they returned with great excitement to the party of searchers to tell what they had found.

The men decided it was not safe to go into the cave. Instead they would try to dam the waters of the river to

drown the giant in his lair. They began to dig earth and stones to build a dam. If they could stop the river Erch from running down into the valley, the waters would rise and fill the cave.

At last the dam was built, the waters rose and began to pour over the rim of the cave. The men watched in fear to see if the creature would come out, but there was no sign of him. The deep cave soon filled with water and they knew that the giant who had terrorised them for so long must be drowned.

You can still see the mouth of the cave if you venture behind the water-fall, but don't go in because the secret black pool is deep enough to drown a giant.

The Girl from Llyn y Fan Fach

In the heart of the mountains in the old county of Carmarthenshire lies a lonely lake called Llyn y Fan Fach. Close by, in Blaensawdde Farm, a boy lived with his widowed mother. His father had died years before, and the boy and his mother kept the farm going as best they could.

One fine afternoon in early August when the boy was watching his cattle on the shore of the lake he saw the face of a girl in the water. He looked over his shoulder to see the girl whose face was mirrored there, but there was no one to be seen, and when he turned back to the lake he saw only the sun glinting on the water and the breeze stirring the rushes. He thought about it all the way home. He was sure he had not been dreaming.

Next day, once again he drove his cattle from Blaensawdde to the lake-shore. It was a fine day and sunlight danced on the surface. He stared into the water hoping to see the girl's face, but this time nothing disturbed its smooth surface.

He turned his head for a while to watch his cows, and when he looked at the lake again, there she was, sitting among the rushes, combing her hair with a comb that flashed gold in the sun.

She was the most beautiful girl he had ever seen. He held out his hand to her, hoping she would come closer, but she stayed among the rushes, combing her long hair. He remembered the bread and cheese his mother had given him that morning, and he took it from his pocket, stretched out his hand and offered it to the girl.

She moved closer to look at the bread he offered her, then smiled and said,

'Your bread's too hard.
You can't catch me.'

Then she vanished leaving scarcely a ripple, and though he waited for a long time he did not see her again. The sun set behind the mountain and the boy made his way thoughtfully home, driving his cattle before him in the dusk.

That night he told his mother about the girl he had seen in the lake, and when he came to the part where the girl said,

'Your bread's too hard.

You can't catch me,'

his mother nodded her head. 'Tomorrow,' she said, 'I'll give you some uncooked dough. Perhaps she'd like that better.'

Next morning the boy returned to the lakeside with the cows, and sat a long time beside the calm water hoping to see her. Hours passed but the girl did not come. Not a sound was to be heard except the distant lowing of a cow on the mountain track, and the soft lapping of lake water on the shingle.

The afternoon had almost gone and the sun had moved towards the west when the waters of the lake began to boil, and he saw her again quite close to him. The boy walked to the water's edge, offering the dough his mother had given him. Her smile teased him and she said,

'Your bread's too soggy.

You can't catch me.'

In a moment she had disappeared into the depths of the lake.

That night, when the boy told his mother the story, she decided to bake another loaf, this time lightly, not too crisp, and not too moist.

The following day a light rain was falling on the lake, and the mountains were shawled in mist as though someone had drawn a thick blanket over the surface of the lake during the night. In the heart of such a vast silence the boy felt lonely and sad. He felt little hope of seeing the girl that day. But still he kept an eye on the lake. Its water was dark and full of mystery.

Then during the afternoon the mist rose, the rain stopped, the sun appeared, and the surface of the water began to boil like molten silver.

He saw her almost at once, a shaft of sunlight shining on her face and hair. He walked straight through the water towards her until she was so close that he could hold out his slice of bread to her. She took it from his hand, tasted and ate it. Suddenly the boy fought away his shyness and asked her to marry him. The girl from the lake thought a while about his question, and at last she smiled and said,

'I will marry you and be your faithful wife until you strike me three times without reason.'

The boy laughed with delight because he knew he loved her too much to strike her, with or without a reason. He took her hand in his, and she smiled.

Then, as suddenly as ever, she vanished into the lake. Was she only teasing him? He waited for a while, perplexed. Then he saw not one beautiful girl but two, as alike as peas in a pod, rising out of the water together and with them came an old man with silver hair.

'You may marry my daughter,' said the old man, 'if you can tell which one of them is your true love.'

The young man looked carefully at the two beautiful young women. They were identical. They had the same hair, the same eyes, the same height, the same little smile. There was nothing to choose between them. He looked for a long time, worried that if he picked the wrong girl their father would not let him marry either of them.

He looked down at their hands. Was there a difference between them? There was none. Then he stared at their feet and as he did so he saw one of the girls move her right

foot slightly. He looked at her, and knew for certain that she was his true love, and that she had moved her foot as a signal to help him to choose her. He walked towards her through the water and took her hand in his.

'You have chosen right,' said the old man. 'Be a faithful husband to her, and remember, if you strike her three times without cause she must leave you and return to the lake. And now, for her wedding dowry she can have as many sheep, cattle and horses as she can count while holding her breath.'

The girl breathed in deeply and began to count.

'One, two, three, four, five!
One, two, three, four, five!
One, two, three, four, five!'
until she had to gulp for air.

The young man could hardly believe his eyes. Flocks of sheep and herds of cattle and horses, a procession of fine, healthy animals one by one broke the surface of the water and waded ashore, shook the waters from their coats and began to graze at the lake side.

After the wedding the young couple went to live at a farm called Esgair Llaethdy, a few miles from the village of Myddfai and not very far from Llyn y Fan Fach. There they lived together in great happiness.

The young man soon realised he had chosen a good wife. She was loving and hard-working, kept the house clean and helped him on the farm. As the years went by they grew prosperous and three sons were born to them. No family could have been happier than the family at Esgair Llaethdy.

One day they had to go to a funeral because a neighbour had died. The church was full of sorrow and tears, but the beautiful woman from Llyn y Fan Fach began to laugh aloud. The congregation stared at her, and her embarassed husband struck her lightly on the shoulder and whispered to her to be quiet.

'I was happy,' she said later, 'because our neighbour has gone to a better place and his suffering is over. But now I feel sad because you have struck me without good cause. If you do it twice more you will lose me.'

Her husband was sorry and vowed to be more careful in future.

One evening some time later, as he was coming home after working hard all day in the fields, he found a horse-shoe on the ground. It was a bright, new shoe which he knew one of his horses had lost, and he picked it up, intending to shoe the horse next day. His wife was in the kitchen but his supper wasn't ready yet.

'Hey! What about my supper?' he asked, playfully tapping her shoulder with the horseshoe.

She turned quickly to him, her face pale.

'That's the second time you've struck me without cause,' she said. 'If you do it once more you will lose me.'

He realised what he had done and made a vow that he would never let it happen again.

For a long time he was careful and they were happy, but one day the couple were invited to a christening. The farmer's wife was not looking forward to the prospect of a long walk. 'We can ride on horseback,' said her husband. So they went into the field to catch one of the horses. That day the horses were frisky and would not be caught. Every time they were approached they tossed their manes and galloped away. At last the beautiful woman from Llyn y Fan

Fach outran her husband and caught one of the horses by the mane. She called to her husband to throw the bridle quickly. He threw it with all his might, and instead of landing at her feet the bridle struck her leg. She let the horse go and stared at him, her flushed face suddenly as ghostly as the face of a stranger. She turned and ran from him like a wild pony, calling the animals as she fled.

'Come Brindle-back, come Speckle-face,
Come Red-flank, come old White-face,
Come White Bull from the prince's court,
Come little black calf,
Come four blue bullocks from the meadow.
Come home, come all, come home.'

The cattle left their grazing and followed her, milking-cows and heifers and calves, the four bullocks and the old white bull, all galloped with thundering hooves after her, and the horses stopped frisking and followed her call as she ran over the fields towards Llyn y Fan Fach. There they all splashed through the water into the depths to disappear below the surface of the lake.

He could not believe she had gone. He climbed the mountain track to the lake time after time, and sat grieving on the shore, watching the water for his beautiful, beloved wife. Sometimes, on summer afternoons when the sun turned the surface of the water to quicksilver, he would fancy he saw her face in the waters of Llyn y Fan Fach. But she never returned to keep him company on the lonely shore of the lake that lies to this day hidden like a secret in its circle of dark mountains.

THE SWORD IN THE STONE

Long ago in the reign of Uthr Pendragon, Britain was a land of warring tribes. Many of Uthr's soldiers had been killed in bitter battles, and one day King Uthr himself was wounded in the head. He lay ill in bed for many months.

During Uthr's illness a baby son was born to him and his wife, and they called the child Arthur. The King's wound did not heal and one day he sent for his chief magician to come to his bedside. The magician's name was Merlin and he was famous all over the world.

'Merlin,' said the King, 'I am dying and I am worried about what will happen to my wife and child when I am gone. My enemies will do anything to stop my son becoming king one day. They will kill him if they can.'

Merlin listened in silence, tears in his eyes. King Uthr spoke again.

'Merlin, greatest wizard in the world. I am giving my child to you. Take him and care for him and do not let my enemies harm him. When he is a man bring him back to the court and crown him king in my place.'

'Lord,' Merlin replied, 'I promise I will take good care of the little prince. I must go away now, but in three days I will return to fetch him.'

Three days later a ragged old beggar-man came to the court asking to see the child and before the courtiers knew what was happening the beggar had stolen the child away. Nobody recognised Merlin in his tattered clothes.

That night, King Uthr Pendragon died.

For many years after the King's death the battles were fiercer than ever among the princes and chieftains of Britain. They needed a king, and plenty of ambitious men were ready to grab the throne that belonged to King Uthr's son, but no one knew where the child had gone.

On the death of the King, Merlin had taken the baby to the home of a good knight called Ector, a loyal friend of Uthr Pendragon, and Ector brought the child up as lovingly as if he were his own son. Ector's son Cai was a few years older than Arthur and the two boys grew up together like brothers until they became strong young men.

Fighting raged across the lands of Britain until at last it was decided that a meeting should be held in London to choose a king. People hoped that a strong, wise king would rule them fairly and put an end to war. But they could not even agree about how to choose a king, and almost came to blows over it.

At last they asked Merlin the Magician to help them.

'Follow me,' he said. He led the quarrelling men to a place where a church stood among smooth green lawns. Close to the church, in the grass, stood a huge stone, and there, buried to its hilt in the stone, was a glittering, jewel-encrusted sword.

'See this,' said Merlin. 'Whoever sets this sword free from the stone will be King of Britain.'

They stared at the strange sight of the bright sword piercing the stone, and some of the men laughed uneasily. One by one the princes and knights stepped forward, took the gleaming hilt in their hands and pulled with all their strength, but to no avail. Not one man could set the sword free.

The men frowned at Merlin for setting this impossible task. Not one of them could do it so no one would

be king. Merlin had tricked them and they would have to find another way to choose their leader.

At last they decided to hold a tournament. They were used to fighting. They would fight each other in the jousting competitions and the man who defeated all the others would be king.

It was a great tournament. Every knight in the land came to try his strength.

Ector brought Cai and Arthur, by now grown tall and strong, to London for the tournament. Ector was too old to compete, and, in his opinion, Arthur was too young, but he allowed Cai to take part.

The morning came when it was Cai's turn to fight and Arthur went with him to carry his shield and his sword. His sword! When they reached the tournament field they discovered that Arthur had forgotten to bring the sword. Cai was very angry and he shouted at poor Arthur.

'I'll go back to fetch it,' said Arthur, and he set off at once, but when he reached the house where they were staying he found the doors were locked and everyone had gone to the tournament.

Arthur did not know what to do. He went to the sword-maker to buy a new sword, but they had all been sold for the tournament.

Arthur walked sadly past the church where, in the smooth green lawn, he saw the huge stone, and buried to its hilt in the stone was a beautiful sword. Arthur took the hilt in his hand and slipped it easily from its stone scabbard. He hurried joyfully to the tournament carrying the treasure to Cai, who was pacing impatiently up and down.

'Where on earth have you been?'

Cai muttered crossly. Then he saw the gleaming sword which Arthur held out to him.

'Where did you get that?' he asked in amazement.

'I found it buried in a stone by the church,' replied Arthur.

Arthur had not heard the story of the sword trapped in the stone and the magician's test to choose a new king, but Cai knew the story, and he took the sword from Arthur and gazed at it in delight and wonder.

'The sword!' cried one of the knights. 'The sword in the stone! This is our new king!'

The knights and princes stared at Cai, who stood holding the sword in his hands and soon the crowd surrounded Cai, calling 'The King! The King!'

For a moment, but only for a moment, Cai was tempted by the glittering jewels in the sword and the sound of the admiring voices calling 'The King! The King!' For a second he was bewitched, then he raised his hand to silence the crowd.

'Not I,' he cried, 'but Arthur freed the sword from the stone.'

The crowd stared at the boy. It was impossible to imagine this boy a king. He was a mere squire, the servant of a knight. An uneasy grumbling broke out amongst them.

At that moment Merlin appeared and on hearing the news the magician knelt on the ground at the boy's feet. The crowd, however, suspected they had been deceived. Had anyone seen the boy do it? They demanded to watch with their own eyes while Arthur pulled the sword out of the stone, as not one of them, all taller and stronger than Arthur, had been able to do it.

'Then we'll go to the church,' said Merlin. 'I will place the sword back in the stone and the boy will draw it out, and all of you will see it happen.'

They returned to the church and the wizard plunged the sword into the huge stone and he asked Arthur to pull it out. The boy drew it out effortlessly.

The crowd was still not satisfied.

'It's easy enough to draw the sword out of the stone for the second time,' they grumbled. Merlin replaced it once more and asked if some of the men in the crowd would come forward to try to pull it out. One by one the knights and princes tried, but not one was strong enough to move it an inch. The shouting and grumbling died away and each man came forward to kneel before Arthur, the boy who was their new king, and who would one day become the greatest king ever to rule Britain.

How did Arthur draw the sword from the stone so easily? There were rumours that Merlin the Magician had something to do with it. After all, long ago when Uthr Pendragon lay dying, Merlin had promised that the King's baby son would grow up to take his father's place as Arthur, King of all Britain.

THE COW ON THE ROOF

Once there was a farmer who was always complaining about the long hard hours he worked in the fields while his wife idled her days away at home caring for the baby, the cow, the pig and a few hens, and doing light work about the house. It was all very well for her, he grumbled, she could stay indoors to play with the baby while he broke his back working in the fields in all weathers, freezing in the heat of summer.
in the heat of the summer.

One day his wife decided she had heard quite enough of his grumbling.

'I'm sick and tired of your complaining,' she said. 'I'll go and work in the fields and you can stay home and do my housework, and care for the baby and the animals.'

Siôn was delighted and he smiled triumphantly.

'That'll teach you! It's high time you knew how hard a man's work is.'

As she left for the fields Mari reminded her husband,

'Don't forget to feed and change the baby, feed the pig and clean the sty, put the cow out in the field, wash the floor and cook the dinner.'

Siôn was hardly listening because he was so looking forward to a lazy day at home doing woman's work while his wife went out to labour in the fields, though the sly little smile on Mari's face made him feel a little uneasy.

As soon as Mari had gone the baby stirred in its cradle and began to cry. Siôn picked up the baby and walked up and down rocking her gently, but she cried harder. He held the baby on his shoulder patting her back and singing to her, but the crying grew louder.

The baby paused for a moment to draw breath for another outburst of

41

screaming, and in that quiet moment Siôn heard another shriek. It was the pig in the sty across the yard screeching for its food. Siôn put the baby into her cot and she cried more desperately than ever. Siôn ran to fetch the bucket for the pig's food. It stood where Mari had put it ready for him in the doorway of the dairy, full of skimmed milk. In his haste Siôn tripped over the bucket and fell headlong through the dairy doorway, and the milk spilled all over the floor. Hearing the clatter of the bucket the pig screeched louder than ever. Siôn got to his feet in a rage and rushed across the yard to the sty, shouting,

'Shut up, you stupid pig, or you can come and get your food yourself!'

Siôn opened the sty door and the pig rushed out as fast as lightning between his legs, knocking him off his feet. Siôn fell flat on his face in the dungheap, and when he stood up he was covered in muck and he smelt like a pig. He looked around the yard but there was no sign of the creature anywhere. He hobbled back to the house, and as he reached the door he could hear a strange sound inside.

The pig was in the dairy where it had tipped up a jug of cream and was lapping it from the stone floor. Siôn lost his temper completely. He picked up an axe from beside the fire and threw it at the pig striking it in the middle of its forehead. The poor creature fell to the floor, dead. Siôn was horrified. What was he to do now? There was no one to help him, with his wife away working in the fields.

Siôn could hear the cow mooing like a beast in pain, and he walked towards the barn, his head spinning. What on earth was he going to do with the cow? He could not take the cow to the field to graze and leave the baby alone crying in the house, and there was so much to be done, the hens to be fed, the floor to be washed, the dinner to cook.

Then he had an idea. Close behind the house there was a grassy slope. The farm roof was thatched with turf, and the brow of the little hill was level with the ridge. 'I can put the cow there,' he thought, 'and if I tether her with a rope she can't wander far.'

He fetched a rope from the barn, tied it round the cow's neck and led her to the grassy slope behind the house. He decided to drop the free end of the rope down through the chimney so that he could be sure that the cow did not wander while he was in the kitchen feeding the baby and cooking a stew for dinner.

He dropped the end of the rope through the low chimney onto the hearth below and went back into the kitchen leaving the cow grazing happily on the little hill behind the house. When he reached the kitchen Siôn washed himself and then tied the free end of the rope round his waist to make quite sure that the old cow could not wander from where he had left her.

He hung the pot of stew on the hook over the fire and began to feed the baby. Things were looking up, he thought. Little did he realise that even worse trouble was brewing.

The old cow had been grazing quietly on the slope for a while when she noticed some juicy green turf growing on the roof of the house. She took a mouthful and it was sweet, so she stepped across the gap onto the turf roof of the house and grazed there for a while. When she had eaten all the grass growing on one side of

the roof she tried to cross the ridge to the other side, but the angle was steeper at the front of the roof and she slipped and fell.

Siôn was putting chopped leeks into the pot of broth on the fire when he felt a sharp tug on the rope round his waist. The next moment he was flying like smoke up the chimney while outside, the cow was sliding down the roof towards the ground. Siôn would have flown completely out of the chimney into the sky but his trousers caught on the hook where the iron pot was hanging. He was stuck, unable to move up or down, dangling in the smoke and the soot, and there he stayed for a long time coughing and sneezing, certain that his end had come. Outside, the puzzled old cow hung from the eaves, her hind feet just touching the ground.

Much later Mari came home from the fields where she had been cutting turnips.

'Goodness gracious me!' she gasped as she saw the cow suspended by a rope from the roof of the house. She had never seen such a thing before in her life, and she ran into the house, stumbling over the corpse of the pig. Her husband was nowhere to be seen, so she picked up the axe and rushed outside to free the cow. She cut the rope with the axe and the cow slid safely to the ground. As Mari freed the cow, she freed Siôn. As the rope was cut he fell down the chimney into the pot of broth.

When she reached the kitchen Mari saw Siôn half in and half out of the pot with a dazed expression on his red face, and the baby peacefully sleeping in her cradle in the corner.

In the end it was Mari who cooked the dinner, and after they had eaten it Siôn went eagerly out to the field to dock turnips, without a single word of complaint.

ARTHUR'S LAST JOURNEY

Many and hard were the battles King Arthur fought and won, until one day there came a battle so bitter that only two men were left alive as silence fell at last on that bloody field. One who lived to tell the tale was Bedwyr, one of Arthur's knights, and the other was King Arthur himself. The king lay on the earth, alive but gravely wounded and Bedwyr ran to his side.

'Bedwyr,' said Arthur, his voice weak with pain, 'many of my finest knights were killed in the battle today. We will never see their like again and my heart grieves for them.'

Bedwyr knelt beside his wounded king.

'Lord,' he said, 'let me tend your wounds.'

'No, Bedwyr. My wounds are deep and nothing can be done. I have other work for you.'

'But, Lord . . .'

Arthur interrupted him.

'Bedwyr, the time has come for me to go . . .'

The knight stared at the king in bewilderment. He did not understand. Where was the king going?

'Now,' said the king, 'I ask you to do one last thing for me. I want you to take my sword, Excalibur, and cast it far out into the peaceful lake which lies beyond the battlefield.'

Bedwyr could not believe his ears. Cast Excalibur into the lake! This magnificent sword was famous all over the world—to throw Arthur's sword into the lake! Surely the king's mind was confused by pain.

Arthur drew the sword from its scabbard and handed it to Bedwyr.

'Go. Cast it into the lake,' he said.

The knight took the sword from the king's hand. He bowed his head to gaze at it as he had gazed so many times before, and once again he

wondered at the fine metalwork and the jewels. Arthur was restless.

'Go!' he said. 'You must cast it into the lake at once.'

The authority in the king's voice made Bedwyr turn and run towards the lake. He clambered over the stones and reached the shore, where he stood talking aloud to himself, gazing at the sword in his hands.

'The king's mind is wandering,' he said. 'Pain has affected his judgment. He wouldn't ask me to cast Excalibur into the lake if he were not gravely injured and I'd be a fool to throw the world's most famous sword into the water.'

He looked at the brilliant jewels and the gold gleaming in the hilt and he knew he could not cast it in.

He hid the sword among the rough sedge that grew at the lakeside and returned to the king.

'Well?' asked Arthur. 'Did you throw the sword into the lake?'

'I did,' replied Bedwyr.

'And what did you see?' asked Arthur.

'Only the wind ruffling the water.'

The king sat up in spite of his pain.

'You are lying to me, Bedwyr. You have not thrown the sword into the water.'

Bedwyr flushed with shame that his king had discovered his lie and that he, the last of the knights, had deceived Arthur.

'Go back and do as I have asked you,' said the king in a weak voice.

The knight ran towards the shore, took the sword from its hiding-place in the sedge and raised it above his head ready to cast it far into the lake. At that moment the setting sun flashed on the jewelled hilt and the precious metalwork of the sword and Bedwyr paused to peer into the depths of the water. The lake was dark and bottomless.

'I can't cast in the sword,' he said to himself. 'The lake is deep and murky and Excalibur will never be seen again if I do. My beloved king is dying and I must keep the sword to remember him. When I tell my children stories about Arthur and the Knights of the Round Table I can take out this famous sword and show it to them. Then they will know that I tell the truth. I will hide Excalibur in the sedge and when Arthur dies of his wounds I will come back to claim it.'

He hid the sword for the second time and returned to Arthur.

The king lay so still he might have been dead, but he raised his head when he heard Bedwyr's footsteps.

'Did you cast in the sword?'

'I did, Lord.'

'And what did you see?'

'Nothing but the setting sun flashing on the hilt.'

'Did you hear anything?'

'Only the wind whispering in the sedge.'

The king's eyes glinted.

'Bedwyr,' he said, 'you're lying to me. Not one of the Knights of the Round Table has ever deceived me before, yet now, as I lie dying, you deceive me. Will you, last of my knights, refuse my final request?'

Bedwyr felt too guilty to meet Arthur's gaze, and tears filled his eyes when he thought of the second lie he had told his king.

He turned at once and ran as fast as he could to the shore, took the sword from the sedge, then, closing his eyes tightly, he hurled it as far as he could into the lake.

When he opened his eyes he saw Excalibur falling towards the water.

Then to his astonishment a pale hand reached upwards from the waters of the lake and took the sword out of the air before drawing it from sight under the surface.

Bedwyr ran breathlessly back to the king.

'Well?' asked Arthur, his voice fainter than ever, 'Have you cast the sword into the lake?'

'I have, Lord.'

'Did you see a sign?'

'I saw a pale hand rise from the water to take the sword.'

A sad smile touched the king's face.

'You've told me the truth at last. Now help me to the shore.'

Bedwyr lifted him to his feet and put his arm around him. The two men moved slowly and painfully towards the water.

Before they reached the lake, Bedwyr saw a beautiful boat sailing towards the shore carrying three graceful women dressed all in black.

'Help me into the boat,' said Arthur.

'Where are you going, Lord?' asked Bedwyr doubtfully.

'To the Island of Avalon to heal my wounds,' answered Arthur.

'I'll come with you.'

'No, Bedwyr, you can't come. No one can come with me on this journey.'

'When will you return?'

'Some day . . . when I am healed completely.'

Bedwyr lifted the king into the boat and the three beautiful women in black received him tenderly. The setting sun gilded the waters of the lake and the sails of the boat before it slipped slowly below the horizon and a night mist shrouded everything.

Bedwyr stood a long time on the shore gazing into the mist, listening to the waters lapping on the shore, alone but for his reflection in the lake's surface. He stood until it was too dark to see, then shivering with cold he turned and walked away into the night.

THE COUNTRY UNDER THE SEA

Today Cardigan Bay is just part of the Irish Sea which flows into the great Atlantic Ocean and waves wash the long arc of its shores from Aberdaron to Fishguard.

To the north the Llŷn peninsula curves its arm about the bay with Ynys Enlli, the island of Bardsey, at its fingertip raising a grey head from the waters. The old princedom of Dyfed embraces its southern shore.

Many centuries ago Cardigan Bay wasn't there. Where the grey seas break, there was once a green country of fertile fields, and there were houses, gardens, villages, cattle and sheep grazing, men and women at their work and children playing. Today that fair country known as Cantre'r Gwaelod lies drowned under the waters of Cardigan Bay.

Before Cantre'r Gwaelod became a beautiful place to live, it had been a huge, land-locked marsh that lay below sea-level, always threatened by flood until a strong wall was built to hold back the sea. At every high tide watchmen walked the wall to make sure the sea did not breach it. If, some stormy night, the sea should find its way between the stones, the watchmen would climb the tower that stood halfway along the wall, and they would ring the great bell. As soon as they heard the bell all the people would come to help mend the hole before the sea could flood their country.

From time to time, when the tide was high and a gale blew from the west, the sea did make a hole in the wall, but every time that happened the watchmen were alert and the people came quickly and closed the breach with heavy stones, so no harm came to their land.

Looking after the wall was such an

important job that it was given to one of the country's most important men. The king of that land, Gwyddno Garan Hir, appointed Prince Seithenyn as Master of the Wall.

Years went by and the seas washed harmlessly against the wall. People worked the land and lived happily in Cantre'r Gwaelod.

One wild autumn night a banquet was held in the Hall of King Gwyddno. It was his daughter's birthday and the king invited the gentry of Cantre'r Gwaelod to the feast. Festivities began early in the afternoon and went on late into the night, and by nightfall Prince Seithenyn had taken too much wine. The prince was drunk.

That night the highest tide of the year was expected and the wind rose quickly and blew strongly from the west. Two young watchmen were walking the wall and looking out to sea. They had waited many hours to be relieved by another shift of watchmen, but no one came. The rest, like their prince, were at the feast and were drunk.

The wind increased to a storm-force gale and the tide rose higher. There ought to have been more watchmen than usual on the wall that night as the hurricane and the high tide together were more than usually dangerous. The two young men walked to the tower half-way along the wall where the great bell would toll if the sea breached the defences. There was no need to ring it yet, but high tide was still to come, so they decided that one of them should go to fetch more men to help with the watch. The watchmen's horses were stabled under the tower and soon one man was galloping through the dusk towards the Hall of King Gwyddno.

The other young guard, a boy called Gwyn ap Llywarch, waited nervously in the tower as night fell fast. The sea was seething up against the wall and white foam filled the air. The boy could hear the waves drumming on the wall and his heart thudded with fear. He thought of the banquet at the hall, and the king's beautiful daughter, dancing at the feast in her finest clothes. Although he was only the son of a gentleman without fortune, he was in love with Mererid, the king's daughter.

That moment, he longed to be at the hall dancing with her.

High tide came. The sea raged and lightning flashed through the darkness, illuminating the waves. Gwyn's companion was a long time coming back, so he ran from the tower and into the stables to make sure his horse was calm.

When he returned to the wall he saw, in a flash of lightning, a sight to set his hair on end. The sea had breached the wall and white water flowed in a wild torrent between the stones. He could hear the rattle of boulders as they shifted with the force of the waves, and the sound of rushing water. The wall had broken.

He ran down the steps and into the tower and hauled the rope of the great bell. It tolled and tolled across the land and the sea and was swallowed by the storm.

But that night no one was listening, no one came to save the wall. Gwyn ap Llywarch ran down to the stables, leapt onto the back of his horse and galloped towards the hall.

He reached the gates of the king's house in safety, and at once he heard a tumult of singing and laughter. Inside he saw an astonishing sight. The king, the noblemen and all the

soldiers were drunk, many so inebriated that they lay snoring and insensible, and Seithenyn, Keeper of the Wall, more drunk than anyone.

Gwyn shouted with all his strength, 'The sea has breached the wall!'

Some of the revellers looked at him, amazed, while others laughed. Where was Princess Mererid? He went to the room where the women were, and saw her flushed with pleasure and dressed in velvet and lace.

'Come with me quickly!' he said to her. 'The sea has breached the wall and is drowning the land. We must get to the hills.'

The smile died on the Princess's face. She looked at Gwyn in confusion. He took her hand and they ran together through the banqueting hall towards the door of the court, and as they went he shouted at the top of his voice,

'Make for the hills! The sea is flooding the land! The wall has broken!'

He ran from the hall to the porch where the horse was tethered, and soon he and Mererid were galloping through rain and wind and darkness.

By now at least some of the revellers understood what had happened and were trying to flee from the sea which rolled over the fields and plains of their beautiful country.

As dawn broke, Gwyn ap Llywarch and Princess Mererid were safe on a high crag over Aber-arth in Ceredigion, gazing westwards over the water. Beside them grazed the tired horse who had carried them safely to the hills. They looked down on a tragic sight. There was no sign now of the great sea-wall, nor of the tall tower that had stood at its centre; no sign of the hall of the king, nor of the villages, the forests, the green fields. There was nothing left but the grey and rolling waves of the sea.

They looked for a long time, tears pouring down their cheeks, until at last Gwyn said,

'Princess, everyone, everything I love has gone. The cruel sea has taken it all. But at least we have each other. We must stay together and build a new home and a new life in these hills.'

'We will, Gwyn,' she replied, and she took his hand and they turned their backs on Cantre'r Gwaelod forever.

The Magician's Treasure

Long ago, in a castle high in the mountains of Snowdonia, there lived a brave prince called Emrys. He was known as Emrys Ben-Aur because he had a fine head of hair the colour of gold and his eyes were the blue of a summer sky.

Those were hard times in Wales. Enemies invaded the country killing her people and stealing their land. Emrys decided he must leave the safety of his mountain fortress to fight for his people, so he set out, leaving the wizard Merlin behind in the castle of Dinas Emrys to look after everything while he was away.

Time went by and there was no news of Emrys. Merlin grew anxious about the prince. What had happened to him? Had he been hurt in a terrible battle? Merlin knew he must leave Dinas Emrys to go in search of him.

Before leaving he decided to bury all the treasures that belonged to the castle, in case robbers came to steal them in his absence. He buried the treasures in a secret place on the mountainside, and then he placed a spell upon the place, saying:

'Let none but a golden-haired boy with blue eyes ever find this treasure.'

He was thinking of Emrys, of course, yet in his heart he knew that the prince would never return to Dinas Emrys.

Centuries passed by, the castle walls crumbled and people had almost forgotten the times of Merlin and Emrys. Only the old ones could remember the story that buried treasure awaited the day when a golden-haired boy would come and claim it. When he came, the old people said, a bell would toll to lead him to the place where the treasure lay hidden, and when he set his foot on the great stone placed over the treasure, it would move aside and the crock of gold would be revealed.

Many young men with yellow hair and blue eyes came in search of the place, each certain that Merlin's treasure was for him, but each went away disappointed. Once, a boy who was as blond as Emrys believed he was on the brink of finding the treasure. When he came to the place where, it was rumoured, the treasure was buried, he picked and shovelled for a whole day until the sun stood on the mountain top and he was too tired to move another crumb of earth. Then he heard the sound of a bell tinkling in the silence. For a moment he stood still, listening. There it was again! He climbed to the place from where he thought the sound came, but the tinkling moved away. Was someone trying to lead him to the treasure? He followed the sound until he saw, standing before him on a rock against the brightness of the evening sky, an old goat with a bell around its neck. The goat bleated against the sunset as if mocking the boy who was so greedy for gold.

Another time there was a yellow-haired youth who loved the daughter of a rich farmer. He knew he had no hope of winning the girl because he was poor. He knew the story that Merlin's treasure would be discovered by a blond, blue-eyed youth.

'I have fair hair and blue eyes,' he thought. 'I will go to the mountains to find the crock of gold. When I find it the farmer will be more than ready to let me marry his daughter.'

It was a fine summer morning and the boy soon reached the place where it was rumoured that Merlin had buried the treasure. He picked and shovelled hard until the sweat poured from him. Afternoon came and he had found nothing, but he was not one to give up easily. After searching for hours in the hot sun, until his strength was almost exhausted, his pick struck a flat stone deep in the earth. Someone must have placed it there. Why? To hide something! He felt his heart thumping with excitement. To hide Merlin's treasure, of course! He forgot his weariness and began to dig again.

Suddenly he felt something move. The earth shook beneath his feet, the air grew heavy and a moment later a flash of lightning cut the sky. He looked about him in fear. The rocks frowned threateningly, the sky overhead darkened as if it were night and a roll of thunder echoed through the crags and precipices of the mountains. He flung down the pick and ran headlong down the mountain to the safety of the valley.

Breathless and with his heart beating as if it would burst, he reached the valley where the sun was shining calmly on the village, beside a beautiful river.

His friends did not believe his story. They had seen no lightning nor heard any thunder that afternoon. Indeed, it had been a beautiful, cloudless day. His friends tried to persuade him to return to the place to show them where he had found the flat stone, but never again would he climb the mountain.

According to legend, no one since that day has searched for the crock of gold, and still it lies under the stone, waiting to be discovered by a boy with yellow hair and blue eyes. One day such a youth will come and, as he sets foot on the stone, it will move back easily revealing the treasure that Merlin hid there so long ago.

What colour is your hair? Are your eyes blue?

The Bee, The Club and The Music Box

Siôn lived with his widowed mother in a cottage in the country. They owned nothing but three old cows which grazed on a piece of land owned by the squire at the big house. They were so poor that they could not even afford to pay the rent for the bit of land, and the squire had threatened to turn them out of their cottage if they did not pay at once.

One night Siôn and his mother were sitting gloomily by the fire. 'You know, Siôn, my boy,' said the old woman, 'we'll have to go to the fair tomorrow to sell our three cows. We must at least keep the roof over our heads.'

Next morning Siôn set out early for the fair, driving the three old cows in front of him. He had not gone very far when he met a stranger on the road.

'Where are you taking the cattle?' asked the stranger.

'To sell them at the fair,' replied Siôn.

'Sell them to me,' said the man.

'What'll you give me for them?'

'A bee, a club and a music-box.'

Siôn saw that the man carried a club in his right hand, a music-box on his back, and, in his left hand, a bee in a little glass box.

'It's money I need,' said Siôn, 'money to pay the rent to the big house.'

'These things are worth more than gold,' replied the stranger.

Siôn looked at the stranger, and at the three things worth more than gold. He decided to take a risk. He took the club, the music-box and the bee in the glass box in exchange for the three cows, and he carried his new treasures home carefully.

'You're home early,' said his

mother, surprised to see him. 'How much did you get for the cows?'

'I didn't get any money. I got these three things instead,' Siôn replied, showing them to his mother. She could hardly believe her ears or her eyes and she burst into bitter weeping. 'You fool! Fool! Where is the money to pay the rent?'

She wept and wept, ranting and wailing until Siôn was almost driven mad. He grasped the music-box and turned its handle. The box began to play the sweetest music in the world and the old woman began to dance on the hearth as if she were a young girl again. She danced and danced until she ached all over and was quite out of breath.

'Stop it! Stop it!' she shouted, still dancing, but before he would turn off the music-box Siôn made his mother promise she would weep and scold no more.

At that moment they heard a knock at the door. The squire had come for the rent.

'Get him!' Siôn shouted to the club which was leaning against the kitchen wall.

The club leapt out of the corner and set about beating the squire mercilessly all over his body. The squire had never known such a terrifying thing before, and he shrieked, 'The rent! The rent!' and wailed, 'Oh! Oh! Oh!'

The next moment he found himself running for his life over the fields to the big house, the club hard on his heels.

Siôn was beginning to believe he had indeed made a good bargain in exchanging the three cows for the bee, the club and the music-box. Twice already the music-box and the club had rescued him from trouble,

and he began to wonder what magical powers were held by the bee in the little glass box. All that night he lay awake, his mind full of wild ideas. By dawn he had made up his mind.

Next day Siôn told his mother of his new plan. He would leave home at once to go out into the world to try to make their fortune. He decided to take with him the magic club and the bee, but to leave the music-box with his mother to help her to defend herself from the squire and his men if they returned to demand the rent.

He travelled for a day and as the sun was setting he came to a fine, big house. Close to the house was a castle with broken walls. Siôn knocked at the back door to ask for a place to sleep for the night. The servants made him welcome and promised him a bed.

In the big, warm kitchen of the house, Siôn asked the servants about the strange castle. They told him that the building of the castle had been going on for a long time, but that in the depths of the night someone demolished the walls which had been built during the day. The gentleman of the big house was so eager to finish building the castle that he had promised that whoever solved the mystery could marry his daughter.

After supper Siôn went out to look at the castle. Big stones lay scattered all over the ground as if giant hands had thrown them. He made up his mind to watch the castle all night long instead of going to bed. If he could only solve the mystery he would marry a gentleman's daughter, and his mother could live out her days like a lady.

At nightfall, Siôn sat down behind a cairn of stones to begin his vigil. The hours passed silently by. He felt very tired and almost fell asleep several times. At midnight he heard an unearthly sound, and by the pale light of the rising moon he saw two huge figures climbing the castle walls. Giants! he thought. The enormous men began to scatter the stones from the walls that the builders had erected the day before, throwing the boulders about like cross children tossing toys.

Siôn rose to his feet, took a stone from the cairn and crept towards the two giants. They were working back-to-back, dismantling the wall. From the shadow of the castle gateway Siôn hurled the stone. It struck one of the giants between the shoulders, and he turned angrily to the other.

'What do you think you're doing?' he shouted.

'What am I doing?' said the other in surprise.

'You hit me with a stone.'

'No I did not!'

They calmed down after a moment and carried on with their work. Siôn took another stone, hurled it as hard as he could, and struck the other giant in the spine. The injured giant turned on his brother in rage.

'You're playing the fool now, are you?'

In no time the two giants were hitting each other—and what a fight it was! Siôn had never seen such a quarrel. They hurled stones and beat each other violently until at last they both lay stretched out on the ground, each with his hands tight round the throat of the other.

The giants lay still on the earth and Siôn waited a long time to see what would happen. At last he realised that they were both as dead as the stones that lay on the ground around them.

When dawn came Siôn knocked at the door of the big house and asked to see the master. After a moment he was invited into the drawing room to speak to the gentleman of the house. Siôn described the night's adventures, his long night's vigil at the castle and the two giants who had been destroying the walls. He told how he had watched the giants at work. 'And now,' he said, 'they are dead and you can finish building your castle without any more trouble.'

'Two giants! Killed!' said the gentleman in amazement. 'But how?'

'That's my secret, sir,' Siôn replied. 'And now I have come to ask your daughter if she will marry me.'

The gentleman looked in horror at the poor, shabby boy. Such a boy as this for his daughter? Oh, no, it was impossible. Still, the boy had killed the two giants who had destroyed his castle walls night after night, and when he looked out of the window and saw for himself the bodies of the giants lying on the ground, he realised his troubles were over. Then he remembered the wild boar which lived in the forest and which had terrorised him and his servants for years. Many had hunted the boar, but the beast escaped every time and had even killed some of the hunters.

'Er,' the gentleman began. 'There is something else you must do before you can marry my daughter. There is a wild boar in the forest that is a terrible trouble to me. I would like you to hunt and kill it.'

Siôn realised that the gentleman was trying to get out of his promise by giving him an extra task, but he said nothing. He turned at once to get ready to hunt the wild boar. First he went to the kitchen to ask for some especially delicious food to take with

him to the woods. He looped a strong rope over his shoulder. That was all. People looked amazed. He was going without a weapon to kill the boar. The boy must be mad.

After walking deep into the dark forest, Siôn placed the dish of roast pork under a great and ancient oak tree, before climbing high into the branches. Then he tied the rope to a strong branch. He made a slip-knot at the other end of the rope and dropped it so it was coiled like a noose around the feast that was laid out on the ground.

From his perch high in the tree he could smell the delicious aroma of freshly roasted meat and sweet herbs rising to his nostrils and it made him feel hungry. Then he heard the sound of savage grunting coming closer and closer through the trees. He had never heard such a frightening sound before. Then he saw the boar. It was a hideous creature with a long, sharp tusk on either side of its muzzle, and its eyes were a burning red. The beast approached the bait under the tree and began to eat it greedily. Suddenly Siôn drew the noose tight over its head and pulled the rope with all his strength. The boar was trapped. As soon as it felt the rope tighten it began to grunt and roar savagely, and it raced round and round in its rage. Siôn was glad he had chosen such a strong branch, and had tied the rope so tightly. The rope jerked till the whole tree trembled and threatened to throw Siôn from his perch to the ground below.

The boar began to tire and his raging and leaping grew less and less until at last he lay quite still beneath the tree.

Siôn climbed down from his branch and ran to the big house to break the news to the gentleman that the wild boar was dead. The squire could not believe it. So many had hunted the boar, and so many had been killed. He decided to send his servants into the forest to see whether Siôn told the truth. The men returned with the news that the boar was lying dead under the great oak tree.

The gentleman's beautiful daughter came to sit beside her father, and when she heard that Siôn had killed the boar she gave him a brilliant smile. Siôn fell in love with her at once. He decided he really would like to marry her.

'Now, sir,' he said to the gentleman, 'about your promise.'

'What promise?' asked the master craftily.

Siôn blushed to his ears. 'Your daughter . . .' he said awkwardly, glancing at the girl, who smiled at him encouragingly.

'Tut!' said the great man. 'You had better forget about her. My daughter cannot marry a poor boy like you.'

Siôn felt anger rise in his heart. He took the glass box from his pocket and opened the lid. The bee flew from the box straight towards the gentleman and stung him on his hands and face. He cried out in pain.

'All right! All right!' he cried. 'You can marry my daughter.'

Siôn whistled gently and the bee returned to the box. The gentleman dared not go back on his word for a second time, and before long there was a great wedding at the mansion. Siôn and the gentleman's daughter were married and everyone was happy.

Sion's thoughts turned to his mother, and the day after the

wedding he took his beautiful young bride to visit her.

When they arrived at the shabby little cottage the door was shut and everything was quiet. Siôn knocked at the door but there was no answer. Worried, he knocked again, and called his mother's name. Then he put his shoulder to the door with all his strength. The door swung open and there, on the floor of the kitchen, they found the old woman lying unconscious and close to death. They called the doctor at once, and after a while the old woman revived. She had not eaten for days and she was weak with cold and hunger. Siôn and his bride cared for his mother for many days, and when she was well again they took her with them to the gentleman's house. There she was treated like a lady. When the building of the castle was finished at last, Siôn and his wife and his mother went to live there together, and they were very happy.

Sometimes, on dark winter nights, when the wind whistled in the castle towers, Siôn remembered the stranger who had given him the bee, the club and the music-box in exchange for three old cows. 'Worth more than gold!' he would say to himself, smiling.

KING ARTHUR'S CAVE

One day a shepherd boy was watching his sheep on the steep slopes of Aran Fawddwy in Meirionydd when they wandered into a ravine choked with dense hazel woods. The boy followed his flock into the gorge, and as he drove them back to the open hill he noticed that a sapling at the edge of the wood had been half snapped-off by the wind. That would make a fine strong stick once it was cut and whittled, he thought. Tomorrow was the day of the Bala Fair. He had already decided to make the long walk to the fair, so he could do with a good new stick to help him on his way. He took out his knife and cut the hazel sapling. After he had stripped the bark and whittled it into shape it made a handsome stick, and the boy felt very proud of it.

When he arrived in Bala the next day, his hazel stick dancing beside him, he found the fair in full swing and the streets thronged with people. He was strolling among the crowd looking at the stalls when he felt a hand on his shoulder. He turned to see an old man with a long white beard and a cloak, woven in all the colours of the rainbow, wrapped about his shoulders. The shepherd boy stared. What on earth could such a fellow want of him?

'That's a fine stick you have there,' said the old man.

'It's not for sale,' said the shepherd suspiciously.

'I don't want to buy it,' said the stranger, 'but I'd like to know where you found it.'

'I cut it from a hazel sapling in a gulley on the slopes of Aran Fawddwy,' said the boy. 'Why do you want to know?'

The old man gazed into his eyes. 'If you will take me to the place I will show you a wonder no one alive has ever seen before.'

The boy was amazed. Was the old man serious? He did not feel like walking all the way back to the slopes of Aran Fawddwy before he had enjoyed all the fun of the fair, but there was a light in the old man's eyes that made him forget all the day's pleasures. He felt strangely disturbed by the glittering gaze of the old man—and no wonder, for in truth he was a wizard. The boy heard himself promise to take the old man to the hazel wood on the mountain, and soon they were on the road to Aran Fawddwy, its silhouette looming larger and larger before them to the south, the bright fair fading into the distance behind them.

The road was long and steep and it was afternoon by the time they reached the narrow valley where the boy had cut his hazel sapling.

'This is the place,' he said. The old wizard knelt on the grass beside the hazel tree and began tearing at the turf with his bony fingers. Soon a black hole gaped in the ground. It was the mouth of a cave. When they had cleared a mound of soil and stones they could see steps leading down into the dark belly of the earth. Before long the hole was big enough for them to crawl through. The wizard took a tallow candle from a pocket in his many-coloured cloak and set a flame to the wick. Carefully, by its flickering light, they descended the staircase cut from the rock until they reached the portals of a vast cavern. A great bell hung at the entrance.

'Mind you don't touch the bell,' said the wizard in a low voice, 'or it will be the end of us.'

By the pale light of the candle they saw a wonderful sight that took their breath away. Hundreds of men clad in gleaming armour lay on the ground as still as death. The wizard whispered that they were the knights of King Arthur, and that they were only sleeping. The boy looked puzzled.

'They will sleep until the bell is tolled to wake them,' explained the wizard, 'but the bell must only be rung if hard times come to Wales. When bitter times return to our land, Arthur and his knights will wake and they will come back to defend us.'

'Times are hard in Wales now,' said the shepherd to himself, and he was filled with a longing to strike the bell and call back Arthur and his knights, despite the wizard's warning. As his eyes grew used to the darkness he could make out more and more detail in the shadows. He could see a circle of stones now, and among the stones lay a sleeping figure, tall and kingly.

'King Arthur!' said the boy, breathless with excitement.

In the centre of the cave was a large cairn of something which glittered in the candlelight. As they moved closer they saw that it was a pile of gold. A strange expression struck the face of the wizard. He ran forward and took fistfulls of bright coins into his horny old hands, gazing at them greedily before dropping them into the pockets of his many-coloured cloak.

'We are rich!' he whispered, filling his pockets with handfuls of gold.

Something stopped the young shepherd from following suit. He looked at the sleeping figure of Arthur in his stone circle, and the brave soldiers dreaming on their shields on the floor of the cave. What if they should wake! That would be a

splendid sight! All rising to their feet together, buckling their armour and their swords to defend Wales once more! Without a word to the wizard, who was too engrossed in the gold to notice, the shepherd slipped away and ran to the mouth of the cavern where the great bell hung. He raised his arms and pulled the rope with all his strength. The deafening gong of the bell broke like an avalanche about his ears. When the echoes died away he heard another sound—the sound of commotion in the cavern, the sound of clattering weaponry, the murmur of excited voices and the clamour of feet.

He heard one voice call out above the others.

'Has our time come?'

Then another voice spoke, quieter but clearer than the rest.

'Not yet, my brave knights. Our time has not yet come. It is only a greedy old wizard after gold, and a shepherd boy who has rung the bell too soon. Sleep, brave knights!'

The shepherd boy heard the clink of weapons laid on the ground, the clatter of shields, then silence as the knights returned to their dreaming.

The boy climbed the steps and the wizard stumbled after him. Night was falling fast as they reached the open air of the hill. The two parted without a word. The boy felt ashamed in the company of the old man who had helped himself to King Arthur's gold, and the wizard too was ashamed that the sight of so much gold had made a thief of him.

The boy set off along the mountain track towards the farm where he worked, and the old man disappeared in the other direction and was soon swallowed by the shadows of the night.

The wizard has never been seen since in Bala or on the mountain tracks of Aran Fawddwy. He vanished as if the black hole in the earth had swallowed him.

The shepherd boy often searched at the foot of the hazel tree in the ravine for the dark doorway that would lead him to Arthur. But search as he would, he never again found the secret stairway that leads to the cavern where the great king and his knights still lie dreaming, to this day.

 The Owl and the Eagle

Long ago when the world was much younger than it is today, a golden eagle, the king of the birds, was sitting on his perch on a mountain crag. All day long he sat alone watching the valleys that spread far below on all sides of his mountain peak. With his keen eyes he could see people and animals moving as small as ants on the broad fields down in the valley, and from time to time the faint calling of man or beast reached his ears, borne on the wind.

The icy mountain air ruffled his feathers, but he only puffed them up a little more to keep himself warm. In the high crags the ravines where the sun's warm fingers could not reach were full of winter snow, even in summer, and few birds flew up to such a barren, lonely place. The eagle sat thinking of the solitary life that befell the king of the birds. It was fine to be king, of course, but sometimes he longed for company, for someone to talk to and share his mountain eyrie. The mountain birds were too stupid—a cackling crow, a flock of twittering starlings—he could not put up with their prattle.

'It's time I took a wife,' he said to himself. 'There must be one among all the birds who is wise and old enough to be queen of the birds and share my crag with me.'

He had made up his mind, and one day he spread his wide wings and followed his shadow down from the crag to the valley below, where trees grew and animals grazed in rich meadows. He glided sedately over the forests, and the small birds were terrified as he passed over them. He circled slowly in the bright air, searching the woods with his keen eyes for a bird old and wise enough to be his mate.

Then, in the valley called Cwm-cawlwyd, he saw a huge and ancient oak tree. In its branches was a white owl whose face was wise and old and beautiful. The eagle hung still on the air gazing at the Owl of Cwm-cawlwyd.

The owl's pale heart-shaped face certainly looked wise—but was she old enough to be his queen? He could hardly fly straight to her branch and ask how old she was. How could he find out?

The eagle flew swiftly south across Wales to the county of Gwent, where there lived an old stag called Rhedynfre. The eagle's keen eyes soon found Rhedynfre the Stag grazing among the red fronds of bracken and grey stones of a hill. He glided down to earth to settle in a thorn tree close to the stag, and he asked if he knew the age of the Owl of Cwmcawlwyd.

'I know her,' said the stag, 'but I'm afraid I can't tell you exactly how old she is. Do you see the oak tree at the foot of the hill? As you see, it's leaf-less and dead, a mere stump which even the spring cannot waken. Long ago, when I was young, it was an acorn which grew on another tree. I remember the day the acorn fell to earth. I remember it splitting open and a green shoot sprouting from it. I remember it as a young sapling, and as a green tree with the moon in its branches, and as a great oak without a single withered branch. It takes an oak tree 300 years to grow to its full height and strength, and the Owl of Cwmcawlwyd was already old before the tree began to grow.'

Then Rhedynfre the Stag folded his long legs beneath him and lay quietly on his bed of red bracken. At last he spoke again.

'There is someone older than I am. Perhaps he could tell you the true age of the Owl of Cwmcawlwyd.'

'Who is that?' asked the King of the Birds.

'The Salmon of Llyn Llyw,' replied the stag.

The eagle climbed the air once more and towed his shadow over the hills until he saw Llyn Llyw like a bright shield below him. He landed on an ash branch that leaned over the waters of the lake, and there was the biggest salmon he had ever seen.

The eagle asked the Salmon of Llyn Llyw if he knew the age of the Owl of Cwmcawlwyd.

'Do you see the scales like pieces of silver on my back?' asked the salmon.

The eagle looked keenly at the great fish and saw the countless scales on the fish's body like a gleaming suit of armour.

'Well,' said the salmon, 'the number of silver scales on my body is the number of years I have lived, and the Owl of Cwmcawlwyd was already old when I first saw her, and nobody who saw her then could remember when she was young.'

The eagle thanked the salmon, and he was about to fly away, because he had his answer, when the salmon called him back.

'Wait, there is someone who knows her better than I do. The Blackbird of Cilgwri. Ask him.'

So the eagle flew over the hills to Cilgwri and there he saw the black-bird in a tall birch tree.

'Blackbird of Cilgwri,' he said, 'you are very old and have seen many things. Do you know the age of the Owl of Cwmcawlwyd?'

The blackbird replied.

'Do you see that pebble at the foot of the birch tree?'

'I do,' replied the eagle.

'You have keen eyes, King of the Birds. You see the tiniest stone. It is so small that a baby's fist would close around it, but I remember the time when it was a huge boulder that 300 oxen could not move.'

'What happened to it?' asked the eagle.

'Every night before I sleep, and every dawn before I sing I polish my gold beak on that stone,' said the blackbird, 'and I have done it every dusk and every dawn of every year of every century as long as I've lived. That's how the great boulder has been worn away to a tiny pebble. I can't count the years I have lived, but when I first saw the owl she looked as old and as wise as she does today, and her voice was no sweeter then than now.'

The eagle had heard enough. He thanked the blackbird for his help, rose into the air and flew straight to Cwmcawlwyd to ask the owl to be his wife.

It was nightfall when he reached the forest and saw the moonlit face of the owl in her tree.

'Owl of Cwmcawlwyd,' he said, 'I want someone as old and as wise as I am to be my queen. Will you be my wife and come to live with me on my crag on the mountain peak, and be Queen of all the Birds?'

The eagle thought the owl would be proud to be offered such an honour, but she was silent for a long time. She was thinking, as all wise people do, before giving her answer. At last, in her shrill, harsh voice, she said,

'Bird of the bare mountains, you live in the lonely peaks where snow lies frozen all the year round. I am a bird of the greenwoods, the secret forests and the shady oak. You are a king. The birds honour you, but nobody dares approach your lonely eyrie. I too live alone, but because I am just a wise old owl the birds respect me. They come to me for advice. If I lived with you on your crag the birds wouldn't fly up to see me. I could share my wisdom with nobody but you. I belong here in the forest, and I must refuse the honour of becoming your wife.'

So the owl refused the chance to be a queen. The golden eagle is King of the Birds, but of all the birds in the world it is the owl who is the oldest, and the wisest, so they say.

GWENLLIAN AND THE PEDLAR

There were once two farmers who were close neighbours and one of them was rich while the other was poor. The poor farmer had three sons called Twm, Dai and Siôn, and the rich farmer had an only daughter called Gwenllian, a beautiful girl with corn-gold hair, eyes the colour of summer skies and cheeks like the roses in her father's garden.

Each of the brothers loved Gwenllian and each wanted to marry her. One by one, Twm, Dai and Siôn went to her father to ask permission to marry her, but the farmer would not give them an answer. Instead he gave each of them a small red calf, each the same age and weight as the other two.

'Whoever gets the best price for his calf in the fair at the end of the year shall marry my daughter,' he said. Each brother left, taking his small red calf home with him.

Twm, the eldest, was a lazy fellow, a harmless, idle youth who liked sitting in the sun chewing a straw better than working.

His brother Dai was quite different. He was greedy and ambitious and he liked to have his own way in everything he did. He would do anything to get the better of others and he was determined to marry the rich man's daughter, and let anyone try to stop him!

Siôn was a fine boy. He was kind and hard-working and Gwenllian liked him best. They loved each other secretly and, whenever they could, they met at night in the shadow of the yew tree in the churchyard. Had the farmer asked his daughter which young man she preferred, she would have chosen Siôn, but in those days girls were not asked for their opinion.

Weeks went past, and Twm's calf died. He was too lazy to feed it regularly, and one morning when he opened the door of the pen he saw his calf stretched out on the floor, as stiff and dead as a plank.

Poor Twm! He had lost his chance to marry the farmer's daughter.

Dai was more careful. His calf grew big and strong. Siôn's calf did well too, and Dai watched it jealously, fearing that Siôn's calf would fetch the higher price at the fair.

As the day of the fair drew closer and closer, Gwenllian too began to worry. She wanted Siôn to win, but she did not trust Dai. She waited her chance to talk to Siôn alone but her father always seemed to be watching her like a sheepdog.

One day her father had to go away, and Gwenllian sent a message to Siôn asking him to meet her that night in the churchyard.

At nightfall they sat talking together under the yew tree. Gwenllian asked Siôn anxiously about the progress of the calf. Was it big and strong? Would it fetch the highest price at the fair? Would Siôn be allowed to marry her? Siôn assured her that his calf was healthy and sleek and that he would marry her and never again would they have to meet in secret in the churchyard.

As they whispered together in the shadows they heard swift footsteps approaching. Had someone discovered their secret? In the pale light of the moon they saw the figure of a young man on the path. It was Dai. Siôn and Gwenllian sat so still they were hardly breathing. Dai walked up to the yew tree and began to cut its branches and when he had cut an armful of yew boughs he hurried away into the night. Siôn and Gwenllian breathed again, puzzled by Dai's behaviour.

Next morning Siôn went to the shed to feed his calf, to find the creature lying dead on the ground.

The boy could not believe his eyes because only yesterday afternoon his calf had been healthy and sleek. In the manger were green branches, and he understood at once. Nothing is so poisonous to an animal as the branches of a yew tree.

He stood stone still and stared at his dead calf, his heart aching with rage and disappointment. His brother had defeated him with cruel cunning and he would lose his beloved Gwenllian.

No! He refused to accept it. In his despair he had a brilliant idea. He turned over the cold body of his calf and began to cut the skin from its body. He dried and cured the beautiful red hide until it became soft leather, then he cut the leather into hundreds of pairs of strong, supple bootlaces.

The day of the fair arrived. Dai took his red calf to the fair, certain that he would get a good price for it, and indeed, he sold it for three pounds, a lot of money in those days. He was triumphant, knowing that his brothers' calves were both dead, and with a light heart he strolled about seeing the sights of the fair. In the middle of a laughing crowd there was a ragged, bearded man selling bootlaces and delighting the crowd with his sweet talk and his jingles.

'String, strong, come along!

Come and buy my leather thongs!'

Everyone wanted to listen to the eloquent tramp and to buy his laces at tuppence a pair.

The fair-day came to an end and people wandered happily homewards talking about the bootlace-seller and singing his jingles.

The laces were strong and supple and all agreed they were the finest laces they had ever bought.

Dai went straight from the fair to the rich farmer's house. As soon as the farmer heard that Dai had sold his calf for a good price, and that the other two calves were dead, he began the arrangements for the wedding. That night his servants cooked a feast for the whole household and Dai took his place at the table between Gwenllian and her father. It was to be an evening of festivity to celebrate the engagement of Gwenllian and Dai, but Gwenllian felt her heart was broken.

There was a knock at the door and Gwenllian got up to open it. There in the doorway stood the lace-seller. He told the company he was tired after walking about the fair all day, and he asked the farmer for a bed for the night.

They welcomed him to the table and shared their supper and the pleasures of the evening with him. At bedtime the bootlace-seller told the farmer he had a bag full of money from selling his laces at the fair, and he asked would his daughter and her fiancé kindly count the money for him before they all went to bed. They all agreed, and soon the money was spread on the table in little piles, and when the coins were all counted the total was announced. Three pounds and five shillings.

Then the bootlace-seller took off his shabby coat and tore off his grey beard, and out of the disguise stepped a handsome young man. It was Siôn.

Siôn told his story: how he had watched his brother cutting the yew branches, how the calf was found poisoned the next morning and how he had skinned it and tanned the hide and cut it into hundreds of pairs of laces, how he had sold the laces at the fair for three pounds and five shillings. He pointed to the piles of bright coins on the table.

The farmer smiled.

'You have won,' he said. 'You have made five shillings more than your brother. It is you, not Dai, who will marry Gwenllian.'

Dai could not argue. He knew he was beaten and he left the house without a word.

Gwenllian and Siôn were married and they lived as happily as any man and wife in the world.

MIST ON THE MOUNTAIN

A young man from Bala was invited to play his harp at a wedding feast at a lonely farm near Ysbyty Ifan. For hours he played his music in the big farm kitchen while the bride and groom and their guests danced the night away.

Midnight struck and it was time to go home. The harper heaved his harp onto his back and set off home across the mountain towards Bala. He had a long way to go and the track was stony, but he was young and strong and he set off with a jaunty stride. The mountains were bathed in the light of a brilliant moon and the night was so clear that he could see every stone on the road ahead.

Suddenly as he reached the mountain pass between Ysbyty Ifan and Bala a thick mist fell. It swallowed everything. The mountain, the road, the very ground beneath his feet completely disappeared. For a while he stumbled on like a blind man, but soon he was forced to admit he had lost his way. Where the stony track should have been there was soft heather underfoot, and antlers of old gorse bushes caught at his legs. Soon he was sure he was lost. He felt his feet sucked into a gluey mire, and before long he was sinking into a bog up to his ankles, then to his knees, then to his thighs. He struggled to free himself, but felt the old bog gripping him even harder in its jaws and sucking him down, down, very slowly, further and further. He yelled at the top of his voice, 'Help me! Help!'

The mist lifted and the moon shone as bright as day. All about him the bog glistened in the moonlight and there, at the edge, was a little old man with a long white beard. He held a coiled rope in his hand, and he hurled it as hard as he could over the marsh, keeping hold of one end. The harper caught the rope and grasped it with both his hands. The little man began to pull the rope, and he hauled with amazing strength until the harper felt himself dragged slowly but surely out of the deadly mouth of the bog.

Soon, solid ground was under his feet and he could have cried with gratitude to the little man who had saved his life. Without him he would certainly have been sucked into the bog never to be seen again. The little man shook his head patiently when

the harper tried to thank him. 'It was nothing,' he said. 'Follow me.'

He gestured, and the harper saw a mansion gleaming like a wonderful ship in the night with lights in all its windows. He stared in amazement. He had never noticed a house like that on the mountain before. He must have strayed far from familiar paths into a strange place.

He followed the little man to the door of the house. The sound of laughter and music reached his ears, and through the bright windows he saw young men and girls dancing. They welcomed him without surprise, brought him clean dry clothes and put a glass of wine into his hands. As he grew warm and merry he felt the joy of the dance fill his heart, and he gazed with pleasure at the company. One girl was called Olwen, and she was the most beautiful person he had ever seen. They danced together, and she moved more lightly than any dancing partner he had known. In such a house, with such a girl, dancing to such music, the harper from Bala thought he was in heaven.

He danced until he was exhausted, and in the small hours of the morning a great sleepiness overwhelmed him. Olwen showed him to his room, and he slept the rest of the night away in the deepest, softest bed in the world. It was like sleeping in a hammock of gossamer.

Dawn broke and still he slept. He had a beautiful dream. In his dream Olwen tip-toed into his room to wake him with a kiss.

He woke suddenly and looked wildly about him. It was not Olwen waking him with a kiss, but a sheep-dog licking his face, and his bed was an old sheep-pen on the mountain. The house had disappeared leaving not a stone behind. He lay at the edge of the dreadful bog where he had almost been swallowed, and his harp was half drowned in the mud. He reached into the bog and pulled it out, its beautiful strings clogged with mire and weeds.

The sheepdog darted away and the shepherd appeared. He stared hard at the boy and his muddy harp. They knew each other, and the shepherd asked what on earth was the young harper from Bala doing asleep in a sheep pen this early morning. The harper told the shepherd about the wedding feast at Ysbyty Ifan, but he kept quiet about the little man and the big house full of light and music and beautiful girls dancing, and Olwen who had danced the night away with him.

The shepherd smiled. 'You drank too much wine at the wedding,' he said. 'You ought to look where you're going. You're lucky to get out of the bog alive.'

The harper said nothing. Nobody would have believed his story anyway, and as he looked over the bog in the grey light of early morning to where the house had been, he found it hard to believe it himself. But someone had certainly pulled him from the bog, and his feet and his heart still ached from dancing, and his head was full of music.

The King's Secret

In a castle at Llanbedrog in the Llŷn peninsula there lived a king with a strange name. He was known as March ap Meirchion, which means Stallion, son of Stallions. King March had a secret—he had the ears of a horse. In spite of his power, his wealth, the servants who waited on him hand and foot, he was an unhappy man. The king was ashamed of his ears. He covered his head day and night so that nobody would ever see them, and he was so careful that the only person in the world who knew his secret was his barber.

The first time the barber came to cut the king's hair, March warned him that he must never breathe a word of it to a living soul.

'If you tell, I'll have your head chopped off,' he warned.

The barber trembled at the thought and promised that he would keep the king's secret safe forever.

The barber stayed silent for a long time, but gradually the secret began to weigh more and more heavily on his mind, and as time went by it grew into a terrible burden in his heart. If only he could tell someone, a close friend, just one living soul, he would feel better, but he kept quiet to keep his head. At last the secret grew into such a dark shadow over his mind that he couldn't eat, and he became pale and thin. One day he went to see the doctor.

The doctor examined him carefully and then he said,

'Something is on your mind. What is it?'

The barber shook his head gloomily.

'I have a secret I daren't tell. If I don't, it will kill me. If I do, I'll have my head chopped off.'

The doctor looked solemnly at the barber and said,

'Go out into the countryside to a lonely place with no living creature in sight, and whisper your secret to the earth. Then you'll feel better.'

Next day the barber went for a long walk alone over the hills. He walked until he reached a lonely place where no living creature, not even a bird, was anywhere to be seen. A vast bog stretched before him, and he walked into its heart, picking his way carefully along a dry path that meandered safely between the wetlands. He knelt down on the earth, and looking nervously about to make sure he was quite alone, he leaned his head towards the rushes and whispered,

77

'King March has the ears of a horse.'

At once he felt so happy that he wanted to sing. If there were little ears listening in the rushes and the sedge of the marsh they would not understand the message, and they certainly could not go gossiping to the king.

The barber hummed to himself as he stepped lightly homewards.

Time passed and the rushes grew tall on the lonely bog. One day two pipers were picking their path over the marsh on their way to the castle to entertain the king that evening, when they stopped at the very spot where the barber had unburdened his heart to the earth. The musicians noticed the tall, thick-stemmed reeds and one said to the other,

'What fine reeds! We could make ourselves new pipes to play at the castle tonight.'

The pipers cut themselves seven or eight of the best reeds. They sliced, notched and shaped them, and when the work was done they went on their way.

At the castle that night all the important people in the land were gathered to listen to the music. King March sat on his throne, his gold crown on his head. When the feast was cleared away the king called the musicians to come forward to entertain the courtiers.

The two pipers stepped into the centre of the great hall, each holding a new set of pipes in his hands. A hush fell on the company as they waited for the music to begin. The pipers lifted the pipes to their lips and blew, but instead of sweet notes, the courtiers heard a voice whisper,

'King March has the ears of a horse.'

The hall was silent for a moment, then a commotion filled the room as people turned to each other in astonishment, unable to believe their ears. Once more the musicians lifted the pipes and tried to play.

'King March has the ears of a horse.' The whispered words filled the hall and everyone turned to look at the king.

In spite of his embarrassment the king was calm. He did not lose his temper. He did not order his soldiers to kill the pipers. His secret was out at last, so he raised his hands to his head and lifted off his crown. At once everyone saw that it was true. The king had the ears of a horse.

Nobody laughed. The people loved March too much to laugh at his shame. He may have the ears of a horse, but he was still their beloved king, and what did it matter if he had the long furry ears of a beast?

March realised that he felt happy at last. He had nothing to hide, nobody to deceive, and he need no longer wear a heavy crown on his head day and night.

One question remained in his mind. How did the reed-pipes learn his secret and whisper it to the court? The next time he had his hair cut the mystery was solved. The barber confessed how he'd whispered the king's secret to the earth to ease his mind, how the growing reeds must have heard the rumour, how the pipers had stopped at the very spot to cut the reeds to make their pipes, and how at last the pipes had told the secret to the whole court.

As the scissors snipped, and the king's hair fell swishing to the floor, the king and the barber laughed and laughed together, two happy men with nothing to hide.

The MAGIC RING

Ieuan lived with his widowed mother in a country village. In the village was a big, dark house hidden by its garden of tall trees, and in the house lived a mysterious old man. Rumour said that he was a wizard and the people were afraid of him. They kept out of his way in case he cast a spell on them.

Ieuan wasn't afraid. He made friends with the wizard, and one day he went to work for him at the big house.

After a while the old wizard fell ill and had to stay in bed, so Ieuan took good care of him, cooked him tasty meals and kept the house warm and clean. In spite of Ieuan's care, the wizard's illness grew worse and one night, when he was at the edge of death, he called the boy to his bedside.

'You've been good to me, Ieuan,' he said.

'You looked after me when nobody else would come near me. I am going to give you a ring to repay you for your kindness.'

He took a gold ring from his skinny finger.

'This is a magic ring. If you wear it on your finger and make a wish, the ring will grant it. Wait until you really need something, because you can only have one wish and then the magic will be finished.'

Ieuan took the ring and put it on his finger. That night the wizard died in his sleep. Ieuan felt very sad. He would miss his old friend.

Ieuan went back home to live with his mother, and he showed her the ring the wizard had given him. Every evening they talked for hours together about how they should use the wish the magic ring would grant them. They knew they must choose with great care because they had only one chance.

Ieuan dreamed of being rich, but his mother shook her head. She had known a few rich people in her time and they had all been unhappy.

'You can't buy happiness, Ieuan,' she said.

The widow would have liked a beautiful house, but Ieuan did not think any house could be a cosier home than the little cottage where he had lived all his life.

So they decided to wait until they really needed something. There was no hurry.

One day Ieuan had to go to the city on an errand. It was a long way so he set off before dawn to walk there, and by the time he arrived the city streets were busy and bright with bustling crowds. He gazed in wonder at the glittering shops full of tempting things, and the window of the jeweller's shop was the brightest of them all. He stared at the necklaces, the bracelets and the rings winking behind the glass. One of the rings was rather like his own.

The jeweller saw the boy looking closely into the window, and he came out and invited Ieuan into the shop so that he could see the rest of his merchandise. Was there anything particular he wanted to buy? Ieuan said he was just looking, and that he'd seen a ring like his own in the window. He held out his hand with the wizard's ring on his finger.

'Yes, I have rings just like that,' said the jeweller.

'No,' said Ieuan, 'there is no ring like mine in your shop. This is a magic ring.'

The jeweller looked curiously at the ring.

'Magic?' he said. 'What do you mean?'

'It will grant a wish,' said Ieuan.

'Well, well!' said the jeweller. 'I certainly have nothing like that on sale here.'

Ieuan and the jeweller talked and time passed and closing time came. Outside it was getting dark.

'You've a long way to go and it's almost dark. Would you like to stay the night, and go home in the morning?'

Ieuan thought of the dark road home from the bright city, and he was glad to accept the invitation to stay.

The jeweller prepared their supper and when they had eaten he showed Ieuan to his room. It had been a long day, and Ieuan undressed, placed his ring on the bedside table, got into bed and fell deeply asleep.

In the next room the jeweller tossed and turned and could not sleep. The magic ring was on his mind. The more he thought of it, the more he longed to possess it.

At midnight, when all was quiet, the jeweller crept from his bed and opened Ieuan's door. He carried a ring identical to Ieuan's, except that it was not a magic ring. He moved stealthily to the bedside table and silently exchanged the rings. Then he left as quietly as he had entered.

In the morning Ieuan dressed and put on the ring without suspecting that anything had happened. He thanked the jeweller for his hospitality and went on his way.

When he was alone in the house the jeweller put the magic ring on his finger and went down the stone stairs to the cellar below the shop. He sat down on the floor and wished for a cellar full of gold sovereigns.

There was a roar, as if a trapdoor had opened to let in an avalanche, sovereigns showered on his head and a golden flood poured down the cellar steps. His wish was granted. The cellar filled to the brim with sovereigns, and the greedy old man was choked to death by his own gold.

Ieuan knew nothing about the death of the thieving old jeweller and he arrived home full of exciting news of the city for his mother. Soon they were hard at work again, feeding the animals on the bit of land that surrounded their cottage.

That night Ieuan said to his mother,

'If we had another field we could keep a few more cows. I could ask the magic ring for the big meadow.'

As usual his mother was cautious.

'Remember, Ieuan, we only have one wish. If we work even harder we can save up to buy the meadow.'

And they did. Together they worked a little harder and a little longer every day until they had enough money to buy the big meadow.

After a while Ieuan began to dream about owning a bigger farm. Should he use the magic ring? His mother reminded him that they only had one wish, so they worked harder than ever and saved until they had enough money to buy a farm. There they worked happily together, and Ieuan grew up to be a healthy and prosperous young man who wanted for nothing.

Every time they wanted something they remembered they could only have one wish in the whole of their lives, so they waited, and worked, and saved, and never, never knew that the jeweller had swapped the magic ring the wise wizard had given to Ieuan all those years ago.

The Story of Gelert

Prince Llewelyn had a hunting dog called Gelert, and there was no finer dog in the land. At home he was a gentle, faithful creature, but in the hunt he was swift and fearless.

On a fine autumn day Llewelyn decided to take a hunting party into one of the great forests of Snowdonia. The prince was accompanied by his wife, his baby son, his courtiers and servants, and they mounted their horses and set out while the frost was still silver on the slopes. All day they followed a great stag over the tree-covered mountains, until at last, at dusk, they cornered the exhausted creature in a forest glade, and killed their prey.

When they had loaded the body of the stag to carry it home to the castle

it was already dark and a new moon had risen to shine in the branches of an oak. The forest was dangerous at night. Hungry wolves wandered the hills and the traveller on a lonely forest road risked his life to bandits and highwaymen.

They decided to pitch camp for the night, and to travel home at sunrise the following day.

At dawn one of the prince's men came to his tent in great excitement. A huge stag had been seen in the forest close to the camp, the biggest stag they'd ever seen. Llewelyn's heart beat a little faster at the thought of another day's hunting, and perhaps a stag to feed them all for many winter months. But his wife was anxious. She felt too tired to ride after the stag, and too frightened to stay in the forest alone with her child and her maid.

The men were already mounted and eager to follow the hounds. Llewelyn was thoughtful for a moment.

'Gelert can stay to look after you. You'll be safe with him.'

'Stay, Gelert!' he commanded. 'On guard!'

The great dog lay down at the entrance to the tent where the baby lay sleeping. He put his head on his paws and lay quietly, his dark eyes watchful.

The sun thawed the early frost and warmed the forest glade. The princess and her maid collected wood for the camp fire, and went downhill to the stream to fill the water vessels.

The baby slept peacefully in his cradle, Gelert stretched out beside him. Occasionally the dog closed his eyes but he did not sleep.

Suddenly a twig snapped in the trees and the dry leaves on the forest

floor rustled under the fall of a foot. Gelert stood up, alert, his hackles rising. A huge black wolf was creeping stealthily towards the tent. Its eyes burned hungrily and it lifted its head to sniff the air for the scent of the child. The dog gave a long low growl of warning.

The wolf moved closer and the dog leapt at its throat. The sun shone down on a terrible battle, white teeth flashing as the two beasts rolled snarling and snapping in the fallen leaves at the entrance to the tent, each trying to seize the other's throat in its jaws. In their struggle they overturned the cradle and the baby prince rolled, still sleeping in his shawl, into a tumbled cloud of blankets behind the cot.

The dog and the wolf fought savagely and neither would give in. Then Gelert, in one powerful leap, seized the wolf by the throat and sank his teeth into its windpipe. He hung on until at last the beast lay still. Gelert let go and lay, exhausted and bleeding, licking his own wounds.

Llewelyn and his men killed the stag and brought it back to the camp. The prince went straight to the tent to see Gelert and his child, and there before him was a terrible sight—the dog was covered in blood, the cradle was overturned, and there was no sign of the baby.

Anguish seized Llewelyn's heart. His dog must have killed his son. As Gelert looked up at him and wagged his tail, Llewelyn drew his sword without a second's thought and struck him with its sharp blade. Gelert lay dead. Then the child whimpered from its mound of blankets behind the cot, and Llewelyn stepped quickly over the body of his hound into the tent. There before him lay the corpse of a black wolf. He snatched his son into his arms, and the baby smiled at him.

Llewelyn ran from the tent with a cry of grief. He had killed his brave and faithful hound and no one could comfort him. He would never forgive himself and never forget the dog he had loved and killed.

Gelert was buried in a meadow beside the river Glaslyn, and Llewelyn had a stone placed over his grave so that all who passed that way through the little mountain town of Beddgelert, the grave of Gelert, would learn the sad story of the dog who died saving the life of a baby prince.

The Land of Strange Names

There was once a farmer who lived alone in the back of beyond. He had no wife, no children, no family at all. He had lived alone for many years, but he was getting older, so he thought it would be a good idea to have a servant boy to help him with the farm and to keep him company.

He looked for a servant, and at last a young boy who had just left school agreed to come to work for him. The old farmer was so pleased to have the lad about the place that he wondered why he hadn't thought of it sooner.

As soon as the boy arrived the old man took him out to show him the farm. Close to the house was a spring where crystal-clear water bubbled out of the earth.

'What a clear spring!' said the boy. 'Such delicious cold water! Does it ever run dry?'

'Never,' said the farmer, 'but we don't call it a spring here. We call it halleluia.'

'Oh!' said the boy in surprise, 'Alright, halleluia it is!' Though he thought it a bit odd.

They crossed the yard to the barn.

'You've got a big barn here, mister,' said the boy.

'Yes,' the farmer replied. 'It's big enough, but it's not called a barn. Mingagor is its name.'

'Oh, ay!' said the boy, beginning to think the years of solitude had turned the farmer's mind.

'Halleluia and mingagor. Well, well!'

They reached the house and went into the kitchen with its flagstone floor and low oak beams. A fat tabby cat slept on the arm of a chair by the fire.

'Move, mwsh-mwsh,' the farmer shouted. Then he turned to the boy.

87

'The word for cats round here is mwsh-mwsh.'

'Oh, yes, mwsh-mwsh.' The boy tried to remember the strange words he had learnt in his new home.

The cat jumped onto the hearth and began to wash herself, and the farmer sat down, took off his boots and gazed into the embers of the fire.

Fetch a bit of wood from the corner to put on the picalhorod, will you lad?' he said to the boy.

'Picalhorod?' said the boy over his shoulder, as he filled his arms with logs. 'Are you talking about the fire?'

'Yes, but the word round here is picalhorod.'

The boy put the logs onto the fire and soon it was burning brightly. The man and boy sat talking by the hearth until it was time to go to bed.

'Well, my lad, it's high time we were off up the gamwydd, I think,' said the farmer.

The boy guessed that gamwydd meant the stairs, so he stood up and climbed the stairs after the old man. The farmer showed the boy his new bedroom.

'Well, lad, here is your sleepbox,' he said, pointing to the bed, 'and there are your ffadindragons.'

'Ffadindragons?'

'Working trousers, boy,' said the farmer.

The boy went to bed and lay thinking for a while about the kind old farmer and his strange language. He fell asleep murmuring to himself all the new words he had learnt.

'Halleluia, mingagor, mwsh-mwsh, picalhorod, gamwydd, sleepbox, ffadin-dragons . . .'

He woke early next morning and went downstairs to make up the fire. In the kitchen he began to chop sticks, rake ashes and lay the fire in the cold grate. He lit the fire, and the dry sticks spat and crackled and sparks flew onto the hearth where the fat cat slept. A spark landed on the cat's tail and at once it began to smoulder. She leapt up from the hearth with a cry and dashed out through the open door across the yard to the barn where the animals' winter hay was stacked to the roof. The smouldering tail of the cat set fire to a bale of hay, and smoke began to billow from the barn door. The boy was terrified. What if the barn, the cowsheds and the farmhouse were all burnt to the ground! He ran to the foot of the stairs and shouted at the top of his voice,

'Mister! Mister! Get out of your sleepbox, put on your ffadindragons and come down the gamwydd at once! The picalhorod has set fire to the mwsh-mwsh, and the mwsh-mwsh has run into the mingagor, and if we don't fetch water from the halleluia to douse it, the picalhorod will burn the lot to the ground!'

The farmer jumped out of bed and into his trousers and ran downstairs. With buckets of spring water they put out the fire in the hay, and then, for good measure, the farmer filled one more bucket and doused the poor cat as well.

Culhwch and Olwen

Olwen was as beautiful as the dawn. Everyone said so. Her hair was the colour of wild broom and her skin as soft as sea-foam. To look at her was to fall in love with her, and every young man in the land would have liked to marry her.

But Olwen had a cruel father who would not let her marry. He was a giant of a man, tall and broad-shouldered, with a big name to match—he was known as Ysbaddaden, King of Giants, and everyone was afraid of him.

Once, years before, Ysbaddaden had been to see a fortune-teller who had told him that he would die on the day that his daughter Olwen was married, so of course he was determined she would never marry anyone.

One day when Olwen was walking with her maid in the fields near her father's castle a young man rode by. His name was Culhwch and he was King Arthur's cousin. The moment Culhwch saw Olwen strolling in the meadow he fell in love with her, and at once he knew that he must marry her. She too, seeing Culhwch, fell in love.

Culhwch rode swiftly to the court of King Arthur to tell the king that he had fallen in love with Olwen and that he was going at once to ask Ysbaddaden for permission to marry his daughter. Arthur was worried when he heard this news. He feared for the young man's life, so he gathered together his bravest knights to go with Culhwch to protect him.

They journeyed on horseback to the giant's castle and at last reigned in their horses at the great door. After much arguing and pleading with the guards they were admitted to the great hall where Ysbaddaden sat on his throne. Seeing a handsome young

90

man surrounded by armed knights, the giant's face tightened in a cruel glare.

'You can never marry Olwen,' he said in a low voice like a snarl.

'I would do anything to win her,' said Culhwch. He looked at the giant without flinching, 'Anything you ask.'

The cruel grimace on the giant's face twisted into a smile. He paused for a moment. This young fellow was King Arthur's cousin, so he had better not refuse him without pretending to give him a chance.

'Come back tomorrow and you can have my answer,' he said.

Next day Culhwch returned to the castle. By now the cunning Ysbaddaden had had plenty of time to think of some impossible tasks for Culhwch to perform before he could marry Olwen.

One by one Ysbaddaden recited a list of thirty-six tasks, and even the easiest one was hard enough to break the heart of the bravest knight in the land. But Culhwch was in love, and when the list was complete he stood up straight and said in a clear voice,

'I will perform every one of the tasks.'

All shook their heads sadly. They were sure that there was no hope at all that Culhwch would win the right to marry Olwen.

With the help of Arthur's knights, Culhwch performed every task. He found Mabon son of Modron who had been lost for a hundred years. He even hunted and killed the terrible wild boar, the Twrch Trwyth. At last there was only one task left, and that was to take the sword out of the hand of Wrnach the Giant. Wrnach never slept and never let his sword leave his hand, and he could be killed only by his own sword.

King Arthur sent two of his finest knights, Cai and Bedwyr, to go with Culhwch to the giant's castle. They travelled for a day until they stood under the looming shadow of a castle built on a huge rock. Darkness was falling fast. Culhwch, Cai and Bedwyr stopped a shepherd on the road.

'Whose castle is that on the tall rock?' asked Culhwch.

'You must be strangers round here,' replied the shepherd. 'Everyone knows it is Wrnach the Giant's castle.'

'Are visitors welcome there?' asked Culhwch.

'No traveller has ever returned from the castle,' said the shepherd, 'so they must be welcome! No one dares go there except the tradesmen.'

The three knights rode up the steep hill to the castle gates and pulled the rope to ring the bell.

'Go away!' a voice bellowed from inside.

'Wrnach is having his dinner and will see no one, except the tradesmen.'

'I am a tradesman,' shouted Cai through the door. 'I am the best swordsmith in the world.'

The porter took the news to Wrnach that the finest swordsmith in the world was at the gate. The giant said,

'If he's that good, let him in.'

He drew his sword from its scabbard and examined it closely. Yes, there were signs of wear—little scratches on the hilt, and the blade was not honed as keenly as it ought to be. Its edge was dull, dented and notched by many battles.

'Open the gates!' he commanded the porter, 'And let him in!'

Only Cai was allowed in, then the gates clanged shut leaving Culhwch and Bedwyr outside. Cai strode across the hall and knelt down close to the giant, and, with an oiled whetstone set to work sharpening one side of the sword while the giant kept hold of the hilt. Cai honed and polished the blade with all his strength until at last the first side gleamed like moonlight. The giant looked at the fine work and he felt pleased. He turned the sword over, and Cai worked hard on the other side of the blade until it flashed like a shaft of sunshine.

'Now for the hilt,' said Cai.

The giant hesitated. No one had ever before taken his sword from his hand, but he saw how dull the hilt appeared against the brilliant, razor-sharp blade, so he let go the sword. It lay for one second in Cai's hand, then he grasped the hilt tightly and with one mighty swipe he cut off the giant's head.

The portals opened and Bedwyr and Culhwch rushed inside. Down in the dark dungeons below the castle lay hundreds of people who had been almost starved to death. Culhwch, Cai and Bedwyr set all the prisoners free and that night, for the first time, there was feasting and rejoicing in Wrnach's castle.

Next morning the three knights went on their way to the castle of Ysbaddaden, King of Giants, taking the sword with them. Culhwch was exultantly happy. This had been the very last task of all, so nothing could stop him marrying Olwen now.

They reached the castle at dusk. When Ysbaddaden saw that Culhwch was carrying Wrnach's sword, his cruel face grew pale and he trembled like a huge oak tree in a hurricane. The King of Giants realised that the love between Culhwch and Olwen was stronger even than he was, and he knew that his end had come, as the fortune-teller had warned that it would. Suddenly grown old and broken, he stumbled away from the great hall.

As soon as he had gone Olwen appeared in the doorway and she ran down the long room to Culhwch. That night they were married, and there was feasting and happiness such as the castle had never seen under the dark, cruel rule of the giant. Happiest of all, after Culhwch and Olwen, were Arthur, Bedwyr and Cai.

THE GOLDEN ARM

Long, long ago in Llanfair, near Harlech, there was once a beautiful mansion and in the mansion lived a rich man called Otto with his wife Helena. The house was full of fine furniture, bustling maids and man-servants, and it was surrounded by the loveliest gardens in Wales. For all their wealth, Otto and Helena found time to be kind and generous to the poor people in the village of Llanfair.

One summer day Otto and Helena were strolling in their gardens which were brilliant with butterflies and sweet-scented flowers, especially roses, their favourite flowers of all. In the middle of the garden grew one enchanted bush, different from all the others, and on this bush just one bloom was open. The couple stopped to admire it, to breathe its scent and touch its silky petals.

'Otto,' said Helena, 'would you mind if I picked the rose?'

Otto smiled. 'The rose will look even lovelier in the hand of the most beautiful woman in the land.'

Helena leaned over the bush and as she stretched out her hand to pick the rose she pricked her finger on a sharp thorn. A drop of blood welled and ran down her hand, but Helena took the rose and forgot about the thorn-prick in her finger.

That night her finger began to swell and turn black and by morning it was plain to see that the cut had turned septic.

The doctor was called, but in spite of his treatment the finger swelled up more and more. At last the doctor said there was only one cure—her arm must be cut off. At first Otto was shocked and he refused to allow the doctor to cut off Helena's arm, but when he saw what pain Helena was in he at last agreed. So it was done.

Helen was heartbroken to lose her arm and it hurt Otto to see his lovely wife without it, so he said to her,

'I will give you a golden arm, Helena.'

He asked a craftsman to make an arm out of pure gold. Soon it was done, and Helena wore her golden arm as naturally as if it were her own.

In spite of the golden arm and all the doctor's skilful care, Helena grew pale and thin and died. She was buried in the family vault in the graveyard of Llanfair church, her golden arm beside her. The most painful moment of Otto's life was when the door of the vault clanged shut, and he knew he would never see his wife Helena again.

Otto's heart was broken and no one could comfort him. He could not bear to live in the house where he and Helena had been so happy together.

'I can't stay here,' he said. 'I will sell the house and everything in it.'

So he sold the mansion, with all its fine furniture and beautiful gardens, and he left Wales to live in a far country. Everybody was sad to see him go.

After many lonely years, Otto married again and he hoped he had found happiness again, though he could not love his new wife as much as he had loved Helena. He spent all his money trying to buy comfort and pleasure but, of course, you can't buy happiness, and in time he was both sad and poor. He decided to go to England.

'There'll be money there,' he said to himself.

He and his wife went to live in London, but poverty followed them. By now he did not have enough money to care for himself and his wife and buy them food and clothes.

So one day he told her that he must go back to Wales alone and that he would be away for a few weeks.

He took a coach from London to Shrewsbury and walked the rest of the way to Llanfair across the mountains.

It was late when he reached Llanfair but the night was clear and moonlit. The village lay sleeping, and nothing stirred. The blacksmith's forge was closed and silent. The door of the inn was locked and the windows dark. The people of Llanfair were all asleep. Otto hated himself for what he had decided to do. Suddenly an owl called from the branches of the great yew tree in the churchyard, and he started with guilt. He reached the gate of the graveyard, opened it slowly, and it creaked on its hinges.

'Gwdi-hoo-hoo-hoo,' called the owl once more.

Otto wanted to run away but having come so far he knew he must carry out his plan. He hurried through the shadowy graveyard towards the tomb where Helena was buried, opened the gate and went in. The coffin had begun to crumble to dust. He lifted the lid and put in his hand. Everything inside had turned to dust except for the golden arm. He took the arm from the coffin and put it under his cloak, then he closed the coffin, locked the door of the vault and hurried towards the open gate of the graveyard. She was there to meet him.

'Helena! Helena! Is it you?'

'It is. I never thought I'd see you do something like that, Otto.'

'But I don't recognise you. Where is your bright hair?'

'Turned to dust.'

'Where has the colour in your cheeks gone?'

'Turned to dust.'

'Oh, Helena, where is the clear blue of your eyes?'

'Dust, Otto. All dust.'

'And your golden arm?'

She gave a scream that echoed through the night.

'It is underneath your cloak, you faithless man!'

Then she was gone and Otto was once more alone. The night was empty and the graveyard silent. Otto walked away, a lonely old man, and all he had left of the wife he had loved was the cold, golden arm he had stolen from her grave.

BRANWEN

One fine summer afternoon the giant Bendigeidfran, son of Llŷr, King of Britain, sat looking out to sea on a crag above the town of Harlech. In the distance he could see a fleet of ships sailing towards the coast of North Wales. In one of the ships Matholwch, King of Ireland, and a large company of his men were on their way to Wales to ask Bendigeidfran for the hand in marriage of his sister, Branwen. Matholwch had heard of the beautiful Branwen, and he longed to take her home with him to the Irish court and to make her Queen of Ireland.

Bendigeidfran would not give his answer at once. He held a great banquet in his court at Aberffraw, and after many hours of discussion he agreed that Matholwch should make Branwen his wife. Soon an even greater feast was arranged—the marriage feast of Branwen, the most beautiful woman in the world, to Matholwch, King of Ireland.

When the feasting came to an end the Irish ships put to sea from the Menai Straits. From the deck of the largest of the ships Branwen watched the coast of Wales fade further and further into the distance until at last it disappeared over the horizon. She was happy to be at her husband's side, but sad to leave her own country.

A year passed and Branwen gave herself willingly to her new life as Queen of Ireland, and when her baby son, Gwern, was born her happiness seemed complete.

Not everyone in Ireland welcomed Branwen, a Welsh girl, as their queen. Some powerful men in the court began to whisper lies against her in the ears of the king. At first Matholwch would not hear a word against his beloved wife, but in time the rumours undermined his trust and he began to believe them. At last the gossip succeeded in turning his heart against Branwen and he banished her from his side in the Irish court, and her baby was taken from her and sent away to be brought up by a foster mother. Branwen was grief-stricken, but even more pain was to come. Her fine clothes were taken from her, she was dressed in rags and sent to work as a maid in the royal kitchens, and to punish her further, the cook was commanded to box her ears every morning.

For a whole year Branwen worked and suffered in the royal kitchen, all the time longing for her child and for Wales and her own people.

Branwen's only friend in Ireland was a starling which came to the kitchen window looking for crumbs. Every day she fed the starling and talked to it until at last a miracle happened—the bird spoke Branwen's name.

One day when the cook had slapped her particularly hard, Branwen dried her tears and took the starling onto her hand, 'Go to Wales and tell my brother Bendigeidfran what is happening to me here in Ireland.'

The starling set out. It flew alone across the Irish Sea, riding the west wind to Wales, and at last it reached the land of Arfon and found Bendigeidfran. It perched on the huge man's shoulder and sang Branwen's name into his ear. At once Bendigeidfran knew that something was wrong with his beautiful sister, and that the starling had brought to him her cry for help.

When he had discovered the full story, the furious Bendigeidfran swore to gather a great army and to sail to Ireland to wreak vengeance on Matholwch and his people for what they had done to Branwen, and at once he assembled his fleet to carry his soldiers across the Irish Sea.

Bendigeidfran was too tall to live in an ordinary house and no ship was big enough to carry him to Ireland. But to Ireland he would go, he was determined, so he waded into the sea, and he was so tall that even in the deepest waters the waves only reached his shoulders. To help the wind to carry the ships swiftly across the wide sea he tied ropes on every one of them and towed them behind him.

One morning, some of Matholwch's servants were looking after a herd of pigs at the edge of the sea, when they saw an astonishing sight. They were so terrified that they left the pigs to care for themselves, and ran to tell the king what they had seen.

'Lord,' said the first swineherd to arrive, breathless, at the court, 'We've seen a terrible sight this morning.'

'What have you seen?' asked the king.

'We saw a mountain in the sea moving towards Ireland, and on the mountain we saw two lakes shining in the sun, and behind the mountain there is a great forest, and the forest is moving towards Ireland too.'

The king could not make head nor tail of the story. He called for his servants, but no one could explain what the swineherds had seen. The story spread through the court and it reached the ears of Branwen in the kitchen.

'I know what the swineherds have seen,' she told the servants. She was taken to the king.

'The mountain the swineherds have seen is my brother, Bendigeidfran, walking through the sea to Ireland to avenge the wrong you have done me. The two bright lakes are his eyes, shining with anger, and the forest that follows him is made of the masts of his fleet of ships, sailing to Ireland.'

When Matholwch heard this, he and his soldiers trembled. They did

99

not want to stay to be killed by the giant Bendigeidfran and his followers so they decided to run away to the west, breaking down every bridge over every river behind them to stop Bendigeidfran and his army. But nothing could stop Bendigeidfran. When he reached the banks of a river, he lay down across the waters like a bridge to let his soldiers walk over his body to the other shore.

At last, the men of Ireland were forced to stop and fight, and a terrible battle followed. Every Irishman was killed and all but seven of the soldiers from the island of Britain died too, and most terrible of all, Bendigeidfran himself was killed by a poisoned spear in his heel.

The seven survivors sailed sadly home to Wales taking Branwen with them, and at last they reached the safety of the mouth of the river Alaw in Anglesey.

Branwen was too unhappy to be consoled. She had lost her baby son, her brother and her husband, and many of her friends. Before long she fell ill and died, and they say she died of a broken heart. They dug a grave for her on the banks of the Alaw, and there she lies to this day, Branwen, the beautiful daughter of Llŷr, under an ash tree where the starlings sing beside the ceaseless weeping of the waters of the river.

GWION AND THE WITCH

Long ago, before the country of Cantre'r Gwaelod was drowned under the waves of Cardigan Bay, before the island of Bardsey had risen from the waters of the sea, when the old oak of Carmarthen was no more than an acorn, when Cader Idris was only a little hill, there lived on the shore of Lake Bala the wisest witch in the world. Her name was Ceridwen.

Ceridwen knew everything. She knew every treasure that lay under the sea. She knew where the veins of gold lay in the heart of the mountains of Merioneth. She could name every star in the night sky. She knew every flower in the fields and woods, and every tree in the forest.

Ceridwen had one son and his name was Morfran. Like any mother, she wanted the best for her child—health and happiness, goodness and wisdom. But Ceridwen wanted one extra, special gift for Morfran. She wanted to bestow on her child the gift of poetry. So she said to herself,

'I will go out and gather a small sprig of every plant in the fields and woods. I will place them all in a great cauldron of water, and I will simmer my brew for a year and a day over a sweet wood fire. At the end of this time the liquid will be reduced to a single, shining droplet. If I place this magic droplet on the tongue of my son Morfran, he will grow up to be a poet.'

Ceridwen set out at once to gather herbs. She filled her arms with them until she could carry no more, and when she returned home with the scented bundles they filled her kitchen from floor to ceiling.

Lavender and camomile,
thyme, mint and lad's love,
hemlock and water-dock,
meadowsweet and broom,
clover, nettle, sea-mint,
thrift and savoury,
pansy and tansy,
feverfew, evening primrose,
belladonna and jack-by-the-hedge,

and many, many more, so many that most of their names were known only to Ceridwen.

Ceridwen called for a great fire to be lit in the courtyard before her house, and a huge cauldron was set over the flames and filled with water. The flames grew fiercer, and a hot, white ash piled up under the cauldron. At last the water boiled and into the rolling liquid Ceridwen tossed the herbs she had gathered. Soon the brew was heaving and the air was filled with a rich aroma.

Ceridwen called her young servant boy, Gwion.

'Fetch me wood from the forest, Gwion. It is your job to keep the fire alight. The cauldron must simmer for a year and a day.'

Gwion worked hard with the help of an old servant. The old man and the boy gathered wood all day long—oak and ash, crab-apple, beech and sweet chestnut. Night and day they watched the branches blaze and fall to a hot, white ash. In the cauldron a rolling black brew simmered.

102

When Gwion began his job stoking the fire under the cauldron, hard frosts locked the earth with a grip of iron and snow was falling on the fields and forests. Weeks passed, and the frost thawed. Rain fell and storms rocked the woods.

Still the pot simmered.

Spring came. Snowdrops appeared, then primroses and wild daffodils.

Still the pot simmered.

Then the hawthorn trees were covered in blossom and bluebells and wild garlic bloomed and the cuckoo called all day long.

The fire burned and the brew simmered.

The sun grew hotter. There were dog-roses in the hedge. There was hay to cut. Gwion grumbled. The old man complained. The pot simmered and the brew was black as ink.

As the seasons passed Ceridwen did not sleep a wink, and Gwion and the old man took turn to stoke the fire. All day they gathered wood and all night one watched the fire while the other slept.

August came. The days were hot. The corn ripened and the birds were silent, their nests empty, the fledglings all flown.

Still the pot simmered.

Berries grew red on the mountain-ash tree and the hawthorn. The first leaves fell. The squirrel gathered nuts for her winter hoard.

Still the pot simmered.

Christmas came, and went, and on the last day of the year, when the trees were bare, Ceridwen slept at last. Winter rains had swollen the streams, and they roared down the slopes of the mountains to fill Lake Bala to its silver brim. That night it began to snow. Snowflakes hissed in the ashes and were turned to vapour in the steam from the cauldron. Gwion raised his axe to a fallen branch dragged from the forest, and he cast the logs one by one into the fire. He looked into the pot and saw that the job was finished at last. The liquid in the pot had boiled for a year and a day and had been reduced almost to nothing. A single, gleaming droplet jumped from the mouth of the cauldron, the magic droplet Ceridwen had brewed for her son, Morfran, the drop of pure gold that would make him a poet. It splashed from the cauldron onto the finger of Gwion, her servant boy.

The scalding droplet hurt Gwion, and he cried out and sucked his finger. Ceridwen woke as the cauldron hissed dry, and she saw Gwion swallow the single drop for which she had waited without a wink of sleep for a year and a day.

Ceridwen jumped to her feet with a cry of rage. Gwion, her servant boy, had swallowed the golden droplet intended for her own son, Morfran.

Sure enough, with one lick of his tongue Gwion soothed his scalded finger and felt a strange feeling fill his mind. Suddenly he knew the names of all the stars. He knew the secrets of space and of the earth, the mysteries of the forests and oceans. He knew the names of all the flowers and creatures that lived on the face of the earth. One look at Ceridwen told him she was after his life.

He turned and ran, with Ceridwen at his heels. Such a race had never been seen before. They ran up hill and down dale, over rivers and through forests. They leapt ravines full of rushing waters and scrambled over steep, snow-covered mountains.

At last, when Gwion was almost

exhausted and Ceridwen was catching up with him, he stumbled.

'If only I were a hare,' Gwion sighed, 'nothing could catch me.'

That moment Ceridwen saw a brown hare bounding over the ground ahead of her where Gwion had been.

In a rage Ceridwen changed herself into a greyhound, her narrow, powerful body travelling so fast that it was no more than a blur. Over rocks and ravines, through bracken and briar, over mountain ridge and along forest track the hound hunted the hare.

When a rushing river lay in Gwion's path he said to himself.

'If only I were a salmon I could swim to freedom.'

The hare vanished, and a silver salmon leapt into the river and began to swim upstream away from Ceridwen. In a flash Ceridwen assumed the sleek body of an otter, and swam powerfully against the current after the salmon.

'Oh,' cried Gwion, as he thrashed desperately through the wild waters, 'if only I were a bird and could escape into the air.'

At once he felt wings grow where fins had been, and feathers cover his body instead of scales. He soared into the air over the river, over the mountain and the forest until he flew above the clouds, too high even for the sharp eyes of a witch. But Ceridwen, too, changed form and became a red kite, rising up, up into the clear air above the clouds. Then Gwion closed his wings and fell like a stone out of the blue dome of the sky into a clearing in a wood. Ceridwen folded her red wings, and dropped after him.

This time Gwion thought he was beaten, but he saw that the clearing in the wood was close to a small farmyard, and in the yard was an open barn, and in the barn was a huge mound of golden corn. The heap contained millions of grains of corn, and Gwion said to himself.

'If I were one of those grains of corn, Ceridwen would never find me.'

He dived into the middle of the pile and became one tiny seed among millions of others.

Ceridwen was furious. She said to herself,

'How will I ever find Gwion in such a huge heap?'

But she was much too crafty to give in now. She decided to become a hen. The little hen pecked and pecked at the heap of corn. It took her a long time and it made her very fat, but at last she had eaten every grain.

'That's the end of that,' she thought, and she waddled home smiling to herself. She had eaten Gwion the servant boy who had accidentally swallowed the magic droplet and stolen the gift of poetry from her own child.

Ceridwen was happy now. Months passed and she grew fatter and fatter, until one day a baby boy was born to her. The child was so beautiful that as she gazed at him Ceridwen could hardly believe her own eyes. A wonderful light seemed to come from his forehead. She looked more closely, then she realised who the child was. It was Gwion! He had been eaten by a little hen, and kept safe as a tiny seed of corn in her crop, to be born after nine months as her own child. Ceridwen was beside herself with fury. 'I'll kill him!' she cried. But as she looked at his face, and he gazed back at her with his sea-green eyes, she realised that she could not bring herself to kill him. Ceridwen put the child into his cradle, and she carried it to the sea shore. Night was falling and the wind had whipped the waves to white foam. She pushed the cradle into the water on the outgoing tide, and watched it rise and fall until it disappeared behind the white crest of a wave to be lost in the darkness of the night.

The storm grew wilder and the waves leapt higher and higher, but the cradle floated all night long like a sturdy little boat. It rose on the crests of the waves, and slid into the deep black troughs between them, but it did not capsize.

At dawn some fishermen, out early to check their nets, noticed the cradle floating on the sea. That morning they had a guest on board. Prince Elffin, son of King Gwyddno Garan Hir, leaned over the bow of the boat and stretched out his hand to catch the floating cradle. He hauled it aboard, and saw, to his amazement, that there was a baby asleep inside.

The baby woke. His shining hair curled round his face, his eyes were sea-green, and his brow glowed with a wonderful light. 'Tal-iesin,' said Elffin. 'Bright brow. That's your name.' The baby smiled.

Elffin's heart was won by that smile, and he lifted the child from the cradle, a treasure from the sea greater than the heaviest haul of fish, or the pearls from the richest oyster beds, or gold from the holds of a fleet of sunken galleons.

Elffin took the child Taliesin home to his father's house. In the court of the great house the child suddenly grew tall and strong as a much older boy. He stood before King Gwyddno and began to sing, making up verses as he went along, and picking out a tune on the harp. King Gwyddno and his courtiers listened in silence to the child poet, and when he had finished they clapped and cheered.

'We have a new poet,' they cried. Never before had they heard such wit and wisdom, such magical words. 'More! More!' they called.

And so Taliesin, the boy with the shining brow, began his long life as a poet, in the court of a king, and his words would last till the end of time.